The Marrying Kind

Judith Anne McCarthy

CRIMSON
ROMANCE
F+W Media, Inc.

Published by
Crimson Romance
an imprint of F+W Media, Inc.
10151 Carver Road, Suite 200
Blue Ash, Ohio 45242

www.crimsonromance.com

ISBN 10: 1-4405-6189-3
ISBN 13: 978-1-4405-6189-4
eISBN 10: 1-4405-6190-7
eISBN 13: 978-1-4405-6190-0

Dedication

To the best of fairy godmothers: Jean and Shirl.

Acknowledgments

I would like to thank Patrice Hannon, Leslie France, and Patrizia Hill for cheerleading me on, reading a drafty version of the manuscript, and encouraging me to write this story and to have fun doing it. A singular thanks goes to Julie Sturgeon, the best of editors, for all of her toil kneading and punching the text into shape. Julie, thank you for the much-needed writing lesson! And, finally, I send a huge thank you to Jennifer Lawler, whose support, guidance, and enthusiasm are indispensable to the writers in her care.

Chapter One

When the tractor died for the fifth time in the two months that she'd been managing the farm solo, Jane O'Hara banged her head against the steering wheel. "Damn it. Not again!" She took off her dirty glove and wiped her eyes with the back of her wrist. She was a good quarter mile out to pasture from the barn, and she had wanted to hog brush the field to plant grass. The pasture was packed down, and had been neglected and oversubscribed. If she didn't intervene soon, it would be mush come spring. She loved the old 1968 John Deere, mostly for his looks, but he was a very bad mechanical boyfriend. "Why do men always disappoint?" It wasn't so much a question as a musical strain that whisked through so fast and lightly, it was unable to tickle enough brain cells to rise to anything articulate, and therefore, no answer could suggest itself. Jane had had enough of relationships that always began with such promise, but then, unaccountably, crashed and burned.

She was an Olympian when it came to suppressing disappointment about men—beginning with her father, whose unforgivable crime had been to die when she was ten. Ever since, she practiced her mental acrobatics daily, hourly if need be. So accustomed was she to the deft choreography required to double-twist past the pain of grief and fear and sadness, she no longer needed her conscious mind in attendance. The emotional tumbling passes and balance required to stick her landings occurred naturally and gracefully, without the liability of too much thinking.

Jane sat on top of the tractor, pulling at the wheel, bouncing in the seat, willing it to start. When it failed again, she took off her baseball cap in a tantrum and flailed at the tractor's narrow gauge panel, just as the Porsche barreled down the gravel driveway to the house. Mark Hannon, she observed with chagrin. "Good grief, could he see me whacking the tractor? Typical," she thought, as she crushed her cap back onto her head.

Jane's pupils had dilated involuntarily when she had first met him in his parents'—her employers'—kitchen. She felt an instant yearning for that warmth that only men provide. And just as instantly, she reminded herself that she was "the help."

Still, he was such a specimen of male perfection. His hair was dark and wavy and in need of trimming. He had probably shaved at some point in the last three days, but when exactly was unclear. His eyes were a deep dark hazel, full of kindness and fun, and his jaw was firm and proud. He had a nose perfectly proportioned to his strong chiseled cheekbones and a determined mouth that seemed poised to laugh warmly, which it did readily and often as he chatted. He wore dungarees and a washed out cotton rugby shirt that showed an athlete's sinewy strength and agility. Reluctantly, Jane relegated him to the same area of her brain that housed Keanu Reeves, the young Paul Newman, and Robert Redford— the unattainable, the forbidden, and the *he's-my-boss!* Besides, she was in a man-vegan state, at the moment.

At thirty-five, it would be fair to say that Jane was beautiful, a woman whose youthful prettiness had blossomed into serious appeal. She seldom attended to her looks, however, other than to appear clean—a challenge in her line of work. She had classic bones, full lips, deep, serious blue eyes that penetrated in their gaze above a neat, straight nose. Her cheeks glowed golden russet from the sun and the outdoors. Her color rose with her emotions, and she often blushed and brightened while she spoke of anything that mattered. She was tall, slim, and what the old horsemen called, "on the muscle." She kept her strawberry blond hair short in a boyish cut, as it was easiest to manage and clothed herself daily in jeans or khakis, which were oversized so that in very cold weather she'd be able to fit thermals underneath. And when she rode or gave lessons, she wore britches and boots. Her best friend Abby often shook her head at Jane and called her choice of clothing "man repellant."

In work boots with a long-sleeve tee and a flannel thrown on top, her dirty baseball cap defending her as best it could against the lowering sun, she felt as unglamorous as a girl who spent much of her day ankle deep in horse poop could feel. When the tractor failed for the seventh time, she slumped over the wheel, which gave her an opportunity to notice just how much manure clung to her boots. She lifted her face to the sun and felt its warmth even as the unseasonably cool September breezes teased her skin into goose bumps.

Jane was hopeful, for what, she wasn't always exactly sure. But hope undefined was her great gift. For despite the incessant calling of the sirens of despair, which she heard all too well and clearly, she had never given up, never let the snow fully cloud her nature. The sun was getting low. Jane would have to leave the tractor out and get the horses in for the night. She patted the John Deere and said, "I know, buddy. You'll feel better in the morning." "Now, why couldn't Mark Hannon see *that*," she thought as she jumped off the tractor step.

When she had filled the last of the water buckets, she stood alone in the quiet of the barn and listened to the horses feed. The muffled swish of hay and the sounds of chewing and snorting, and the sweet smell of cedar shavings, straw, and fresh manure soothed her. It was the most perfect time for Jane. The sun was nearly gone, just a few passionate streaks of red left at the horizon, and the horses safely stabled for the night.

She made a mental note to talk to the New Jersey extension service about red clover. It caused the horses to incessantly drool harmless, but disgusting slobber—so that they looked alien-possessed. She'd arrived at the farm during slobber season, and hoped to avoid it next summer.

It was a far cry from her urbane days in college academia. She'd loved teaching, but hated publishing and, frankly, she wasn't overly fond of the majority of her colleagues. Never had she met such a congregation of self-involved, pretentious, gobbledygook-speaking, nail biting, humorless misfits—who didn't have the sense to fold their hands and sit quietly, but had instead to be full of passionate intensity. In the beginning of her career, she thought she would be making a difference introducing young minds to great literature. But she became disenchanted. The literature she thought was great had become passé. And the literature her colleagues admired was, in her opinion, unreadable.

In the end, she feared she'd become as moldy as the department's old guard—Stewart Parless, for example, who haunted the ivy halls with ivy of his own growing in lush abundance from his ears. Or the yeasty remains of Andrew McKayne, who may have been brilliant in his day, but had become incoherent and dissipated, and never failed to offend any woman within earshot. His jacket was untouchable, bearing the skid marks of museum-quality jelly doughnut smears and coffee spills. "Give me slobber, anytime," thought Jane.

She longed to do something brave and different, and very much in keeping with her childhood bliss. After her father died, her mother worked double shifts to keep a roof over her and her brothers' heads. Jane was free to pretty much do as she pleased, young as she was, and that meant hanging out with the horses on the farm where her parents rented their house. At eleven, she learned to muck out, groom, and tack up. She threw saddles on horses whose withers were above her head. She tightened girths and held horses for other children as they mounted. She made herself useful in a hundred ways, and in exchange she was given riding lessons. Perhaps if her father had lived, he'd have paid for the lessons. But probably not, they were poor then, too. Her mother had told her often that she weighed the relief she felt that she knew where Jane was against the dangers of her hobby. In her exhaustion, relief won out.

Gray Goose, the boss mare and a wise old horse in her own right, stomped a foot and hung her head over the stall door. She seemed to size up Jane smartly, her good, honest eyes beckoning Jane nearer to stroke her head and neck. Jane listened to the horses in perfect peace for a while longer as they went about the business of merely being. How calm they were. How safe they felt. She could have stood there for hours on end, but she still had a lot to accomplish. "No rest for the weary—or is it the wicked?" she muttered to herself.

She cleaned the tack from the day's lessons, listened to messages, swept the barn, checked the horses once more for hay, and topped off their water buckets. Then she went to the house and fixed herself some soup and toast. Tomorrow was a big day: she'd organize the farrier and the vet, give her lessons, get the young horses going, and hope the old John Deere would start.

Afterward, she was to meet with the Hannons and their son, Mark, for dinner.

Chapter Two

Nora Hannon was a smart, trim woman in her sixties, with thick white "angel" hair. She had always wanted a large family, but no other children had followed Mark. When she and her husband, Robert, bought Hannon Farm, Mark was already grown into a young man. So Nora created a riding academy that welcomed children from all backgrounds to her farm. They were the children of her heart.

Jane had come for her interview for the stable manager position on a hot August afternoon. They met in Nora's "office," a spacious parlor in the house, the imposing structure in which the Hannon family lived. There they went over Jane's resume and application and why she wanted to take on such a physically demanding job. Jane wanted to feel herself pressed again, she explained. She was fit and the work had anchored her and given her a sense of purpose and security from childhood through her undergraduate years. "Working with horses made me feel stable, as it were," she laughed shyly, "I'd like to feel that way again."

For the self-conscious pun alone, Nora hired her on the spot. Jane was to have complete managerial say over daily operations, and Mark would be on board to help her with any cost-related issues. In Jane, Nora sensed a passion for the farm equal to her own. For despite her great wealth, Nora loved the work. "You are always budgeted to hire whatever professionals you need. Please don't think you have to do all the mucking yourself—it's ridiculous," she had insisted, even though Nora mucked out daily and knew Jane would, too. "Use some of the men, Jane. God knows, we've got plenty of them hanging around the place—and believe me, they're well paid."

Nora saw much more in Jane than a farm manager, however. Accustomed as she was to looking at every young woman as a possible wife for Mark, she secretly hoped to add mother to her grandchildren to Jane's duty roster in due time. She was exactly the kind of girl Nora believed Mark needed. He was bright, handsome, an athlete, and a determined professional, but damn it, he was emotionally arrested, and Nora wanted grandchildren.

She had waited patiently for Mark to outgrow his youthful passions and settle down, but he seemed just as determined to remain single. Recently, she had observed the first gray hairs appearing at his temples. He favored Robert, who at sixty-seven was still gallantly tall and handsome. The two looked cut from the same cloth, but she hoped Mark would become a father before his entire head became silver.

Mark was a brilliant investment lawyer, a financial genius, and was wealthy in his own right. He had been running the family farm and holdings since he'd completed law school. Her successful, handsome son, she sighed inwardly. She regretted having gotten rich and not having had more children. These two circumstances, she believed, had formed an aloofness in Mark's character: He was too damn independent.

She never openly criticized or pressured Mark. She shared her thoughts sparingly even with Robert, who'd often said, "Let the boy alone, he'll find his way in the end," though even Robert showed signs that he was beginning to have his doubts. Clearly, Mark liked women. But however different his girlfriends were from each other, Mark slipped away from each of them in short order. One month, he'd be seeing a college student, dangerously close to being young enough to be his daughter. The next month, he'd be intrigued by an uptight commercial Realtor, more driven by her work than Mark was by his. Then there was the bohemian artist, who might have panned out but for her valium addiction; and on and on went the list. The only thing they had in common was that they were all pretty. And that seemed to be all Mark required.

Women fluttered in and out of his life every few months, so that Nora lost track of them. Far from being the kind of mother who thought no woman good enough for her son, Nora rather believed almost *any* woman was good enough. She admired her own sex and disapproved of Mark's seeming inability to make a commitment. She wondered where she and Robert had gone wrong. Why was her son still single? Why was he unable to form a serious bond with a woman? It bothered her that Mark was...a cad. And lately, she had begun to wonder, "What's a little valium addiction among friends?"

When she'd met Jane, she thought, "Here is a great woman. Beautiful, spirited, strong," and hoped that if she placed Mark and Jane together, something would come of it. Jane met Mark's only observable criterion: She was fabulous looking. Nora was confident she'd at least make the first cut.

As they rode out on the farm together in the hot weeks of August, Nora observed Jane's quiet confidence juxtaposed against her charming lack of self-possession. Whatever Mark's commitment issues were, Nora hoped Jane would solve them. She determined to do what little lay in her power to bring it about and formed a simple plan and dreamed of the beautiful children Mark and Jane would make.

Chapter Three

Out of curiosity, Mark had Googled Jane after their first meeting, and found an impressive array of scholarship. Though he had minored in English as an undergraduate, he majored in political science—more masculine. The subtleties of Jane's approach to T.S. Eliot, therefore, eluded him. Still, he was smart enough to recognize a strong mind and a confident competence in her work.

At dinner, Mark's parents had dropped their big news on them: Nora and Robert were moving on to life's next adventure, leaving him in charge with Jane to oversee the daily operations. Mark was surprised, but pleased on two counts. First, he was feeling corralled in New York, and secondly, because Jane, now that he'd met her, was a damned attractive woman. He was intrigued.

Over the next few weeks, they were thrown together frequently to discuss the farm, expenses, staffing, and the like, and they naturally began to get better acquainted. And Mark, no stranger to the stable and its routine, enjoyed taking his exercise in chores as often as his work permitted. While they spoke freely and often, neither brought up personal matters, but they became more relaxed in each other's company. Mark found Jane intelligent, funny, easy-going, and likeable. Likeability plus a healthy male appetite and Jane's beauty equaled Mark wondering what it would be like to be her lover. Of all the women Mark had set his sights on, he had never considered a woman in a subordinate position. Not even his administrative assistant in New York, who clearly worshipped him and was cute, too. But, she did not present nearly the temptation Jane did. Still, common wisdom dictated that one not get his apples where he got his oranges, whatever that meant. He couldn't stop himself from fantasizing, however, which he didn't think would harm anyone.

Mark was accustomed to casual and easy relationships with women who took things for what they were worth, at least out of the gate. He didn't want to wrestle with his conscience or lead anybody on—but far more importantly—he didn't want to get tied down. I-n-v-o-l-v-e-d. It always surprised him, therefore, when his relationships with women became serious from the woman's point of view. And that seemed to be the persistent pattern and was happening again with his latest girlfriend. So, he jumped at his mother's invitation to make an extended visit to the farm. He needed to retreat from New York for a while and let things simmer down. He hadn't planned it, but he couldn't help his attraction to Jane. Of course, he wanted to tumble in the hay with her, if she were willing, but he did not need to push anything. He'd just let things happen spontaneously, if they were to happen at all.

The Hannons threw an annual grand party at the farm, which satisfied their many professional obligations. Mark had an extensive client base among Hollywood actors, directors, and writers. And man, those people liked to party! The farm and office staff, townspeople, and local merchants were always invited as well. Nora even invited all the lockjaws, who, while they might look down their noses at the nouveaux riche Hannons, would never quibble with fame and excellent wine.

With Nora and Robert leaving, the party duty fell to Mark. He intended to get Jane involved too and asked her to come to the house. Indeed, Mark had quickly and unconsciously gotten into the habit of thinking of Jane as the woman of Hannon Farm. He often sought her input on matters that he regarded as needing a feminine perspective. And he had also just hired a new man, Mac, whom Phillips—the house manager—had recommended. He wanted to ask Jane to take him on in the stable. And he wanted to get cracking with the party plans, too. But even more than these solid reasons for asking Jane to the house, he simply wanted to see her and was glad of the excuse. Mark briskly attended to his business matters, raced through phone calls, skypes, and emails, and feeling more at leisure, called Jane and invited her to the house.

Chapter Four

For her part, Jane was glad of Mark's invitation to come to the house as well. She too had been enjoying Mark's company, their easy friendship, and the playful banter they had quickly developed. She also wanted to tell Mark that the John Deere was acting up again. She sat on the mounting block with a hoof pick to get all the packed straw, mud, and horseshit out of her boots. Then she stiff brushed them dry and walked down the white gravel road to the house, which rose up out of the landscape heavily and imperiously. She trotted up the steps between the grand Grecian pillars and rang the bell.

"Good morning, Jane," said Phillips. "Mark is in the library. He's expecting you." Phillips was not much older than Mark, but he had an old soul. Jane felt positively complimented that he used her familiar name, while he was always just and only, "Phillips."

"Thank you, Phillips. How are Mary and the assorted minor Phillipses?"

"Oh, quite well, thank you. Mary still talks about the macaroni and cheese casserole you brought her after Peter's birth. She's tried to make it more than once, but says she can't get it to taste the way it did when she brought the baby home, though I can't tell the difference."

"Well, you know what they say: a great dish begins with a great appetite." ("And an undiscerning palate," Jane gently mused.) "I'll call Mary later and share my mac and cheese secrets," and headed down the hall. "I'll let myself into the library."

Jane knocked lightly and opened the library door. There had been an unusual cold snap as September spilled into October, of which Mark had taken full advantage and had a blazing fire going. "Hello, Jane," he called out cheerfully from behind his papers. He rose up to greet her with his hand extended.

"You don't want to shake hands with me, Mark," she laughed, "I've been mucking out stalls all morning."

"Don't be silly," he said as he took her hand in both of his and turned her palm up to examine it. "Uh-oh, what have we here? Your career line says, 'She was only a stable girl, but all the horsemen knew 'er.'"

"Very funny, Mark. I have one for you: Your John Deere is stuck in the field again. When are you going to make me a happy woman and buy me a new tractor?"

"Have you been abusing it again? I've got a sentimental attachment to the John Deere, Jane. It came out the year I was born. He's like a brother to me."

"Well, your brother needs rehab," Jane offered, ignoring the fact that she routinely beat the tractor and kicked its tires. "I would like to hog brush the fields and plant grass in the next couple of weeks. Or your pretty pastures are going to look like mud slabs come spring—your mother will kill us both."

"Jane, you're such a hard woman to please. Why don't you ask for fur coats or diamonds? With you it's all tractors, and hay, and pastures. Still, you're right about my mother." He let her hand fall, then sniffed his own hand, "Yummy, horse poop."

"I told you," she exclaimed, laughing with embarrassment and wiping her hand on her sweatshirt. "So, what did you want to see me about?"

"Couple of things. First, I hired this new guy—his name's Mac. And, I'm sorry I didn't ask you first, but I told him it would be okay if he helped you out in the stable," he said, quickly and almost wincing.

"A helper? Me? Don't you think I'm doing a good job?"

"Of course you are, Jane, it's not anything bad about you. The guy's had it rough—he has PTSD and was on the street for a million years, and he asked if he could work with the horses. He's a veteran. I didn't have the heart to say 'no.' There's something about him,

Jane. He's got this uncomplaining, suffering thing…" As Mark described Mac, Jane felt her shoulders relax. She was a sucker for strays, of all species, and was pleasantly surprised by Mark's concern for the unfortunate Mac. It made her like Mark even more.

Jane glanced from Mark to the window and scratched her nose. She squinted back at him and was about to speak when he added, "You know that Hanoverian stallion you fell in love with? I bought him. He'll ship next week. I was going to surprise you."

"Well now, I *really* can't say no, can I? Well played, sir," Jane laughed. "Does this Mac even know anything about horses?"

"I assumed he did when he asked to work with them. I guess we'll find out. He speaks Spanish," Mark lamely offered.

To which Jane teasingly laughed, "Oh, why didn't you say so! He can give the horses Spanish lessons, and I'll teach them lines from Shakespeare, and it'll all be grand," and then thinking out loud—a habit she had, which utterly charmed Mark, "well, I can actually use the help, especially with the stallion. Pretty soon, I'll be bringing *all* the horses in at night, and that's a lot of poop to muck," and then turning to Mark, "Actually, if this Mac knows anything about horses, the timing is great."

Brightening, Mark said, "Now, don't kill me, but I've got another favor to ask."

"Not killing you is already another favor. You only get three— anymore and you'll be over quota. You'll have to toss one back," she said playfully.

"This last one is fun. It's that time of year when Hannon Farm hosts a fall party," Mark said. "It's both a tradition and an obligation: My mother always planned these things, and now the duty has fallen to me. And when I say 'me,' I mean 'you and me.' It won't be difficult—we've hosted this party for twenty years, so it's pretty self-performing. I have a list of to-do's, but I need you in the loop so you can make decisions in case I'm not here. Would you mind? My assistant is good with smaller events in the city, but

I'd really like a partner here at the farm. Are you game? I promise it won't take up a lot of your time."

Jane was excited by the prospect of a party at the farm. "Are you kidding? I *love* Halloween. It's my favorite holiday next to Christmas." She immediately suggested a good, old-fashioned masquerade ball, "We could have a hayride with the new tractor, and everyone can come in formal costumes. It'll be great fun, and good PR for the farm," she said excitedly.

"Let's call it 'The Dragon's Ball,' she said. "The locals and their kids, and your clients will love it. And, the whole party could be coupled with a charity fundraiser. We could have a headless horseman appearance—oh, Halloween is just so much fun!"

Jane was pleased when Mark agreed to a Halloween theme. She glanced at her watch and told Mark she expected Ben, the farm vet, in a few minutes and asked if they could discuss detailed party plans later.

Mark, reluctant to end their meeting, threw out the first jest he could think of, "By the way, Jane, I could use those Shakespeare lessons. We shouldn't let all your training go to waste."

"You're on," she called back over her shoulder, "but I expect to be paid—you can balance my checkbook for me."

On her way back to the stable, Jane smiled. She enjoyed teasing Mark and their easy bantering. And she felt she'd glimpsed another layer in his personality—he was a definite softie. She knew he was a fierce businessman, but she liked that he genuinely seemed to want to help people, like this Mac guy, and that he wanted her to be happy, too. After all, he was her boss. He didn't have to ask her permission to hire anyone and was free to assign him wherever he wanted. But he did ask her. It made her feel that she mattered, that she wasn't just some subordinate. She was also happy about being asked and trusted to help plan a party with him, even without reading too much into his having said he wanted a "partner." And she was happy because it was a fine, clear, crisp day. She set a brisk pace back to the barn, smiling all the way.

Chapter Five

Mark didn't think there was any harm in asking Jane to dinner at The Tavern in Gladstone so that they could plan the party in earnest. He knew most of the vendors they would need, and his mother had left a list of contacts for him—which decorator she'd used in the past, which talent agency for music, who to use for invitations, and the like. Phillips would take care of the consumables. But Mark wanted to get Jane's ideas, too. He wanted her to feel included. Her enthusiasm was infectious—she'd already conceived of a great theme for the party—and he thought it would be nice for her to get off the farm for a change.

He decided not to call her on the cell, but to walk about until he ran into her "accidentally." He needed a walk anyway and headed toward the stable first. He couldn't stop himself from laughing at the image of Jane instructing the horses in soliloquies from Hamlet, while Mac translated into Spanish.

Mark, who had never known any material want, who was a beloved only child of great parents, had a keen admiration for those who had been less fortunate. He had found Jane uncomplaining— she was no one's victim. But he had also come to know that she'd been very poor, raised by her mother with her two brothers, and that she'd been self-supporting after high school. She impressed him. He had never had to triumph over any of the challenges she had faced. He found himself wanting to ease her life, if he could, if it was within his power. He thought people like Jane and Mac and Phillips were the ones really worth knowing. People like my parents, who had made their fortune from nothing. He, too, had made his own money, but he'd been given every advantage to do so, and he knew it.

He saw Jane in the adjacent outdoor riding arena, finishing a lesson. "Okay, drop his head, and give him a nice rub on his neck, and tell him what a good boy he's been." As the young rider crooned to her mount and dropped the reins to let him walk out, Jane gave the English Setter, who stood patiently by her side a quick obedience lesson. The dog had come to the farm as a gift from a family who found his energy levels too high. On the farm, he could run free, swing home for dinner, and cozy into the farmhouse with the Golden Retriever and the big mutt at night.

Jane had adopted them all out of the stable where they'd been living, and had been training them. The setter, whom Nora had named Vincent, was the most intelligent of the crew. The retriever was Dega, and the big, ridiculous-looking mutt was Frankendog, Frank for short. "Sit, Vincent," Jane commanded and then laughed and roughed his neck when he obeyed. Mac had started in the barn earlier that day and was throwing the night's hay down from the loft. "Heads up," he bellowed, though no one was below.

Mark leaned on the fence and watched Jane finish the lesson for both rider and dog. "Don't tell me you're actually civilizing that hound," he called out to her.

Jane smiled and waved back at him and said, "He's very smart—I have to spell words like o-u-t so he doesn't get too excited."

"Ah, but is he balancing your checkbook?"

"No," she said, strolling toward him, "but then neither are you."

"Well, bring it to dinner, and I'll take a crack at it."

"Dinner?" she cocked her head.

"Well," he said awkwardly, "I thought since you're helping me with the party, it was the least I could do. I mean..."

"Oh!" she stammered, mortified that he might think she was insinuating that the invitation was some kind of date. "Dinner to plan the party. That would be great. When did you have in mind?"

"If you have no other plans, tonight," Mark suggested.

"That works for me—what time?"

I know you get up at the crack of dawn," Mark said, "so, early—how about seven?"

"Great. Do you want to drive together or meet there?"

"I think we can drive together without compromising our reputations. I'll pick you up at quarter to."

Mark was pleased that Jane would have dinner with him and looked forward to getting to know her off the farm. Mark had seen a lot of women in britches and boots and thought Jane stacked up with the best of them. She managed to look utterly feminine, no matter what she had on. Even oversized khakis could not conceal her athlete's firmness. He admired her capable strength and discipline. He never would have thought that any of the dogs, especially the hyper Vincent, would attach to anyone. He'd seen enough Cesar Milan episodes to know that Jane must have a gift for gaining an animal's trust. He tucked this insight into the enlarging area of his mind reserved for observations about Jane O'Hara.

Chapter Six

Jane hurried through the afternoon feeding and barn chores and asked Mac to top off the water buckets. She hurried to her farmhouse, showered, and threw on black dungarees, a black jersey, and topped it with a little leather biker jacket. Rushing around brought color to her cheeks, and she ran downstairs when she heard Mark ring the doorbell.

When they were finally seated at The Tavern and had ordered dinner, Mark said, "So, let's talk Dragon's Ball. What do you have in mind?" and took a small notepad and pen from his inside jacket pocket.

"Let's see, Halloween parties can be fairly inebriating affairs where I come from, so have you thought about accommodating your guests for overnight, if need be?"

"I'll hire a limousine service for the New Yorkers," Mark said as he made a note. "The locals are on their own."

"What about music? Good bands book up pretty quickly."

Mark made a note to contact the talent agency his mother used and asked Jane, "Should we go with classical or rock?"

"Classical?" Jane was incredulous. "On Halloween? Big bands can be cool, but most people will prefer your classic rock, don't you think?"

"Let's do both swing and rock and alternate?" Mark offered.

"I like the cut of your jib," she said. "What about food? I'm guessing Phillips arranges that?"

"Yes, Phillips will contact vendors he's used in the past and will present us with menus and costs. I'll eat anything, so, you can choose if you like. Oh, and if you could help the decorator with decisions, I'd really appreciate that. I'm lost at that kind of thing."

Jane said, "I'd be happy to. I love decorating. We should also put out some personal touches—you know, your favorite bubbling cauldron, pumpkins we carve ourselves. Phillips' kids might enjoy carving pumpkins, which reminds me: will there be a lot children at the party?"

"The locals will bring kids, but they'll leave early. The New York crowd will definitely leave the niños at home—besides, most of them are single or between marriages. Maybe we could offer a prize for the best kid's costume? Scholarship money for their college fund or something," Mark suggested, "my clients don't need the money, but a lot of the locals aren't so rich."

Again, Jane warmed to Mark's feeling for those less fortunate than himself. He really was very sweet, she thought. "Definitely," she said, remembering how difficult her own college funding had been. "Oh, and how about a bachelor, bachelorette 'match' for charity? You know, everyone who is single tosses their name in a bonnet and cap, and the matches are made by drawing."

"That's a great idea. My clients can afford ten grand apiece, or they can stay on Match. Maybe we should make them put in their Match pictures—you know, woman on the beach in a wet suit with her Italian Greyhound—like that doesn't tell a story!" Mark joked.

"You've been reading my profile, I see," Jane laughed, and then quickly added, "Just kidding—I'm not actually on Match." ("Yet," she added, under her breath.)

"So what charitable causes do you like, Jane? What should we support?"

"Oh, anything with animals or kids is fine with me—as long as I don't have to watch the infomercials," she added.

"I know, right?" Mark exclaimed. "The sight of Marlo Thomas makes me bawl like a baby." Switching a gear, Mark said, "I'll throw in fifty, providing I don't have to throw my name in the hat."

"Are you kidding? You're on last month's cover of *GQ* with Leonardo DiCaprio for God's sake. You have to be a contender. But I'm exempt," Jane laughed.

"No way. It's your idea—you're in, missy. Hey, wouldn't it be a laugh if we drew each other?"

As the waiter set down their meals, Mark asked if there was anything more that Jane could think of that would ensure the success of the party. She paused thoughtfully and said, "How about a gypsy fortuneteller? I have a girlfriend who gives psychic readings. I could see if she's interested. She's very serious about the ethers—or is it the vapors?"

"That would be outstanding. Can she tell us when the market will get freaky or who's going to win the Super Bowl?"

"Rachel doesn't have that kind of connection with the spirits, Mark. She's more of a character reader. But she's eerily good at it. Believable and kind of spooky. Even I have a hard time being alone with her sometimes. I mean, I love her to death, but sometimes she freaks me out—*like my future lies naked before her*," Jane said, in her wooo-wooo voice.

"Even better—and, I'm not gonna lie: the idea of one woman's anything lying naked before another is kind of arousing," he grinned.

Jane, caught off guard by Mark's innuendo, smiled and blushed and quickly looked down at her plate, at a loss for that sassy, saucy comeback that would have come in so handy. Instead, she was Jane, the postulante, the novitiate, the nun-bun in the oven. For Pete's sake, she thought. Say something.

Mercifully, Mark threw her a rope, laughing warmly, "I'm sorry, I'm a guy! You can't say 'naked' to me without my inner twelve-year-old coming out." Without skipping a beat, he resumed the gypsy topic, "It wouldn't be Halloween without a fortuneteller on deck. I hope your friend can come."

Jane asked whether Mark had thought about security, and said,

"I think Mac could knock some heads if you need him to. He's an ox."

"Good to know," Mark said, "I'll ask some of the men to keep an eye on things, too. But it's not typically a violent crowd."

They ate for a few seconds in silence. Mark piped up, "Can I ask you a really personal question?"

"Sure, but I may decline to answer," she warned.

"Have you ever been married?"

"Alrighty then, that *is* personal," she laughed and added, "Nope, I've had a couple of near misses, but no, never married. What about you?"

Mark laughed, as Jane had come to know, easily and often. He shrugged, "No marriages, no near misses, even. I guess I never found the right girl," and bit the matter off with a smile.

*

Mark didn't drop Jane off until nearly nine, and while she didn't want to be rude, her days began at five-thirty a.m. He had insisted on walking her to the door, however, and then asked if she would let him come in, just for a minute, to see the place, as it had been a long while since he'd been inside the old farmhouse. Jane had enjoyed their dinner so much, she agreed, figuring she'd just have to sleep harder and faster.

"Would you like a beer?"

"Perfect," he said. "You know, this house is my mother's favorite. She always says she'd rather live here than in our house. She says that about all the little places she fixes up on the property, but she means it with this house. My parents lived in it, you know, while they were renovating the big house. I was in college then." Mark looked at Jane and asked, "Are you happy here, Jane?"

"Oh, yes, most definitely. Your mother certainly went to pains to bring this place forward," Jane observed. "It's really the most extraordinary house I've ever lived in. It has all of the charm of an old farmhouse, but modern and comfortable at the same time."

Jane's tastes in furnishings resembled Nora's: lots of picture rugs, overstuffed sofas and chairs, and all of the flourishes that made her house seem cozy and warm. She led Mark through the foyer and living room, past her favorite leather club chair, down the wide hallway, and into the thoroughly modernized kitchen.

"The place looks great, Jane. It's so...homey."

"You can thank your mother—she insisted on new appliances and of course most of the really good antiques she had acquired. I brought a few old pieces, and the newer furniture is mine. But your mom really has an artist's eye for interior design."

Surveying the room, "It looks like you belong here," Mark said as he relaxed against the island counter. Jane turned to him from the refrigerator, and as she offered him his beer, he took her wrist in one hand and slipped his other around her waist and pulled her close to him. He didn't strong arm her. His touch was more of a suggestion, a request really, to come to him. "Jane," he smiled softly and kissed her. He felt her unresisting acceptance of him as she melted into him. He deepened the kiss. He felt her yielding to him, matching him, their hearts beating together as he settled into the kiss, which both had good reason to stop, but neither did.

Mark had been leaning against the island counter, but he turned her so that her back was against the counter and continued to press himself against her even as he held her close, bending her backward over the counter, forcing her hips to rise toward him. He felt her body liquid and warm as he held her tightly, burying himself in her curves and exploring her with all his senses. He bent her further back on the counter, so that she clung to him, and he felt her warmly inviting him.

Jane, for her part, had had more than a few first kisses, but none like this. Mark breathed into her, gently filling her lungs. Her mind, so frequently full of unnecessary, often self-critical chatter, went blank—blissfully, wonderfully blank. She drew him ever more deeply in. She held onto him. She didn't want to let go. She wanted this kiss to go on forever.

Gradually, he eased off and looked at her, his eyes smoldering and dark. He rested his forehead against hers for a moment, kissed her again lightly and whispered her name, "Jane." After a few seconds, he rasped, "I'd better go."

She steadied herself against the counter and barely had the presence of mind to speak, but she heard herself huskily babble, "Okay." She cleared her throat. The earth had just shattered, like a sheet of ice and she was falling, but he had to go so, "Okay." Still dizzy, she choked, "Thanks for dinner," not knowing what else to say.

Mark pivoted and left abruptly. Jane, still holding the beer, didn't know what to make of it. She stood leaning against the island while her head cleared. Typically self-effacing, she had not thought him attracted to her, not in that way. They flirted, and he was truly nice, but she had not expected an attraction, for the obvious reason that he employed her. Until that moment, she didn't know how much she liked him, how much she had wanted him to kiss her, and then left her. *Dear God, what a kiss!* It was just as well that he'd had the sense to stop. She was ready to let him take her on the kitchen island. She thought, "You can't think of a saucy comeback at dinner, but you'd drop your drawers in the kitchen? Oh, sweet Sister Lucille…" Jane took a few sips of the untouched beer, and then dumped the rest. She was tired, but also excited and perplexed. She rethought her man-vegan status, and sleep eluded her for quite a while. She reviewed and analyzed all of her interactions with Mark to date. She really didn't want things to get complicated. But it was too late for that.

*

Mark dove into his car. "What the hell was that?" he remonstrated with himself. Like an alcoholic or drug addict who had convinced himself that he could be in the presence of a drug and not pick it up, he had deluded himself into thinking that he could go on as Jane's friend and not try to touch her. All of his high-mindedness about being her boss certainly flew out the window. It wasn't two minutes before he was all over her like a hobo on a ham sandwich. Not that it wasn't wonderful. It was amazing. She was amazing. And clearly, she was ready for him.

But now he'd opened precisely the can of worms he'd determined would get him into no end of trouble. He wasn't afraid of a sexual harassment suit. He knew Jane wasn't the type of girl who would scheme a kiss into a lawsuit. But, that intimate kiss that spoke so loudly all the things Mark had been tucking away in his mind, would now lie between them whenever they met like a cartoon sign that would go ignored: "danger, no hunting, no fishing, no trespassing, go no further, stop now, turn back, life as you know it is over." He hated for things to be awkward for Jane. He'd have to apologize to her. He was her boss, and he'd crossed the line. He didn't want a relationship, and yet that is what he'd opened the door to. It was unfair of him. He'd taken an advantage.

Later in bed, Mark rehearsed thoughts about Jane. A single neural pathway in his brain vibrated the thought that he was seeking to get out of something that hadn't even begun yet. And, for a moment, he glimpsed something about himself that he didn't like, but didn't yet know how to remedy. So, the thing went unnamed and settled back down into a dark recess. It was a long time before he was able to drift off, and as he did, he experienced Jane's warm and accepting kiss and felt his chest and guts ache.

Chapter Seven

Jane couldn't wait to talk to her best friend, Abby. Abby worked in history department in Van Dyck Hall, right across the mall from Jane in the English department. They'd first met at a student admissions committee function and had liked each other immediately. They were hardly more than undergraduates themselves, having both rapidly sped through their graduate study programs, Abby at Harvard and Jane at Princeton. They had both grabbed the brass ring in landing tenure-track jobs at a major public university. And Jane the more so, as she was locally grown.

Through the years that they earned their tenure, they provided mutual consolation and solace over the many indignities they'd endured at the hands of students and senior colleagues. As non-tenured faculty, they could not afford to offend anyone, despite innumerable petty provocations, like the time Jane's department chair, who suffered a classic case of inflated ego ("pedestalitis," Abby called it), had sneeringly asked her if she'd been a "women's studies" major as an undergraduate. This because she'd had the temerity to suggest that Melville had a "thing" for Hawthorne. Jane sucked it up, back peddled, and later commiserated with Abby.

And then came the day within a week of each other, that magical day when they learned that their tenure packets had been approved and they'd both been recommended to the university administration for promotion. Abby was thrilled, and Jane was depressed. That job that she'd worked so hard to achieve, that her mother had waitressed double shifts to help her achieve, seemed a poor recompense for the effort. Jane had lost her enthusiasm for teaching, her colleagues' insufferably petty politics, all the departmental, gossipy in-fighting, and she began to look for a way out. Jane, who had worked her face off for tenure, felt like a proud fifty-seven Chevy truck amidst a bunch of Buicks (Cadillac wannabes).

Abby, petite with little hands, little feet, and big eyes, often struck Jane as a doll. Her child-like features belied her strong and agile mind. She was a consummate performer, and approached life as staged art. She was an able historian, not because she was so bright (though she was) but because she played her hand so smartly within her department. Whereas Jane always felt an imposter when she hid her feelings from her more powerful colleagues, Abby was genuinely approachable. She accepted people as they were, warts and all. Always bubbly and cheerful, Abby simply didn't have any meanness inside of her. She told Jane that being a Jew had taught her that the world was full of anti-Semites, but she just couldn't hate them all. She was appalled by violent hatred, but blundering ignorance only inspired her to educate.

Jane couldn't imagine religious or ethnic persecution—even though she was second generation Irish-Catholic. She remembered that once a child in school had called her a "Mick," and paused for the fiery retort she'd intended to provoke. Unfortunately, Jane didn't get the memo that she should find being called a Mick insulting and just went blankly on her way.

Abby and Jane shared in each other's holidays. Both were more spiritual than religious. Jane hadn't set foot in a church since her confirmation, and Abby's upbringing had been very liberal. They educated each other light-heartedly about Yom Kippur, Hanukah, Rosh Hashanah, Christmas, Lent, and Easter. Abby took Jane to temple, and Jane took Abby to midnight mass at Christmas, a fairly mortifying adventure since neither of them knew how to conduct themselves liturgically, and Abby kept saying in a pronounced voice—"Wow! I can't believe I'm in a church!"

But more than anything else, Abby and Jane saw each other through their various relationship trials. They had each fallen in love a few times, dumped men, and had gotten dumped by men. And throughout the years, they upheld each other's self-esteem.

It was great that Abby was still close by, and Jane wanted to catch her up on everything, the Halloween party, the date that was not a date, and that kiss. She also wanted to invite Abby to the party and to ask if she thought Rachel wouldn't mind playing the gypsy palm reader.

Rachel and Abby grew up together, like sisters. Jane loved Rachel almost as much as she loved Abby. But unlike Abby, Rachel was austere, mysterious, quiet, and quite mesmerizing, though with a wicked sense of humor. She was the most physically beautiful woman Jane counted among her friends and acquaintances. A few inches shorter than Jane, she was slender, with thick, curly dark brown hair, that if extended reached down to her waist. Rachel had given up trying to drag brushes through it. She just let it cascade in ringlets and pulled generous portions of it back to expose her exquisite complexion. Rachel had the kind of true beauty that both Abby and Jane envied. At parties, everyone wanted to know who "that stunning woman" was.

Still, Rachel struggled with prescience all of her life. Evidently, it came to her from her Aunt Sylvie, who also had "the gift," which Rachel referred to as "the curse." Lately, she had reconciled herself to having insight, and had begun to discipline her mind so that she might provide more accurate readings, rather than the muddle of images and incoherent prognostications and metaphors that often emanated from her attempts.

In addition to her physical beauty, her "gift" could be a bit unnerving. When Jane first learned of Rachel's abilities, she wasn't sure she could be friends with her. But, as she got to know her, she relaxed. Sister Lucille would have boxed her ears, though, if she knew that she'd made friends with someone who had the "sight."

Though she talked to them by phone, Jane had not seen her two friends for over two months. In fact, the last time she saw them, they had come over to her apartment so that Abby could "talk sense" to Jane about how crazy she was to dump her career in the toilet.

"I'm not dumping my career in the toilet, Abby, I'm taking a sabbatical."

Abby looked at Rachel for support. "Rachel, can you do anything with her?"

Rachel replied, "Honestly, I can't. I don't think Jane is doing anything wrong" and added to Jane, "it's your mother," just as the phone rang. Jane checked caller id, but needn't have. Rachel continued, "Actually, Jane is making the smartest decision of her life." She closed her gorgeous hazel eyes that seemed to change in color, depth, and hue depending on her mood, from pale translucent brownish green to a deep emerald, and in rare instances a light sea green.

"I see your sun, Jane. Your day here is brightening to a crisply clear, perfect fall day. There is warmth, and just the right amount of chill and breeze, and your sun begins to approach its zenith. I see a wonderful afternoon unfolding for you." She opened her eyes, and the deep sea green of them began to fade back to a clear emerald. "There are obstacles, shadowy and indistinct, but formidable. Still, I know you will be happy, no matter what."

"Really honing the gift, I see," Jane said wryly. "I mean could murky be that vague for me?" But she appreciated the positive vibe in any case.

Now, she couldn't wait to conference them, yet when she got them both on the phone, she didn't know precisely how to begin. Rachel interceded, "Jane, I was telling Abby that it's high time we came out to your farm and spent some time with you. Do you intend to invite us?"

"Of course. That's one of the reasons I'm calling. Abby, you can commute from the farm to school—it's only forty-five minutes—but Rachel, can you get away from the city?"

Abby gleefully interjected, "It's perfect, Rachel. You can come to my house by train, and we can drive from Highland Park to Bedminster."

"Yes, and I know you've already Googled the directions," Rachel offered.

"You cannot hide from prescience, Abby," said Jane.

"Yes, well, that and Abby told me she planned to Google them last night, and we were going to demand an invitation if you hadn't offered one. As for me, my work travels with me. So, I'm good. My clients can always reach me on the cell. Besides, I'm looking forward to spending time in the country. I'm ready for a change of venue."

"Perfect," Jane said, "because I was hoping to talk you into playing gypsy palm reader at a major Halloween party Mark Hannon is hosting."

"Oh my God!" said Abby, who knew the kinds of parties Mark threw from her addiction to the tabloids. "Oh, Rachel, it will be so much fun. Say yes, say yes!"

"Are you kidding? Of course, yes!" Rachel agreed. "Playing gypsy at Mark Hannon's party might kick something off for me outside of the city." Rachel didn't care for Tarot cards or conventional paranormal paraphernalia. She preferred to create drawings or pastels as she read for her clients. The artwork often reflected the reading, and frequently clients bought her art. It was, after all, inspired by them.

But Rachel sensed the spark some anxiety from Jane, "There's more you're not telling us right now, yah?"

Jane let the silence play out for a few moments before answering, "Yes, there is. But I want to tell you in person—so when can you get here?"

They decided that Friday would be a great day to come for their visit to extend for as long as they wanted. Jane couldn't wait to let her friends help her figure things out.

Chapter Eight

Mark went back to New York briefly. He decided he'd rather risk the wrath of his ex-girlfriend, Veronica, than see Jane at the moment. He couldn't help being rich, good looking, healthy, and personable. And he tried and almost always succeeded in being the best man he could be. He was naturally attractive to women. And he loved them, at least superficially. He was used to all things being equal in his relationships, which was to say mutually convenient. Mark had never had to struggle for anything. He was privileged, he succeeded in his own business ventures, and there seemed an endless trail of women who wanted to be with him.

He didn't use women. He just didn't start a relationship with the headline, "I'm not the marrying kind." But how does one disclose that anyway, he wondered. Is a guy supposed to say, "just so you know, I'm going to make your toes curl, but I'm never going to marry you. So, howsaboutit, you want to get going?" That kind of takes the mystery out of things. And besides, he wasn't against marriage, not at all. He assumed he would marry…someday, just not now. There was plenty of time. He was still young, he told himself.

Jane troubled him, though. She worked for him. She'd be the one to suffer if she got in too deep with him, and he didn't want it on his conscience. Jane, who did not seek him, and yet who opened so sweetly when he asked. Jane, who embarrassed so easily and enchantingly. Of course, he'd never fire her or hold her job over her head. Good grief! He wasn't Simon Legree. But she might feel the need to move on if things went badly from her perspective. Mark did not want her to have to face that choice. He escaped back to New York to think of what he could do to repair things and kicked himself for having gotten, out of necessity, into damage-control mode.

He raced from the limo to his building. He shot glances up and down the sidewalk, half expecting to see Veronica stalking him. She'd called innumerable times, and he had not returned her calls, believing that silent running was the kindest way to end things. Best to stay off the radar was his thinking. Phoebe, who had introduced him to Veronica after an Armani shoot in which she'd styled Veronica, had chided Mark, "Do you have any idea how buggering the silent treatment is? Give the girl some closure for heaven's sake, Mark!" But Mark believed that any communication would only encourage more communication, and would just prolong her unhappiness. It was better to let her get on with things on her own, he thought and so ignored Phoebe's advice and Veronica's countless calls.

At twenty-five, Veronica was exciting. She had unusual features that, though not precisely beautiful, leaped off the photographic page as absolutely stunning. And she was not stupid. She knew how to dazzle and was fully prepared to capitalize on her looks for as long as she possibly could. Initially enamored of Mark's holdings more than of holding Mark, she'd seduced him so deftly that he'd imagined the idea must have been his.

But despite her sophistication, Mark managed eventually to uncover what was obvious to everyone at first glance: Veronica was fond of Mark, but if he'd been a poor man, she would never have wasted her time. Her jaded view of men, coupled with Mark's innate misgivings about commitment, doomed the relationship before it could ignite. Mark, always quicker to realize when it was time to cut bait, dumped her still wriggling on the hook. The momentary guilt he felt passed. He salvaged his sense of personal integrity believing that if things weren't right for him, they couldn't be right for her either. With this infallible logic, he proved his innocence and rested his case.

Mark collapsed gratefully into his leather office chair and swiveled to look at the cityscape. He surveyed the concrete buildings, the reassuring edges and surfaces that were so simple and reliable. His thoughts returned to Jane, and after a bit, he persuaded himself that he was making too much of it—it was just a kiss, and he convinced himself that Jane was without doubt untroubled by it, and he should not trouble about it either.

*

Back at the farm, Jane, reflecting on that kiss, was shocked by the suddenness of her desire. She tried to put the kiss out of her mind, but it had made a groove in her brain that she kept falling into. She had already concluded from experience—more ample than she liked to admit—that she wasn't good at relationships. She had been so grateful for the job at the farm, where she could just be herself by herself. She was afraid that getting involved with Mark would end badly, forcing her out her job, the county, and possibly the state.

When it came to men, part of Jane was always on the alert, always that little girl she had been, who had loved and needed her father so badly, who was so utterly desolated by his death. That little girl's voice that never rose to full consciousness in Jane urged her in inaudible whispers to be very careful and to remember how much love can hurt. "Even the best of men leave," she whispered in her blood.

As she tossed hay for the night, she was unaware of the precise nature of her turmoil, only that she felt off. She did not have thoughts and feelings, so much as they had her. A vague sort of sadness and dread played at the edges of her emotions. She drove the clouds away, as she had always done, by focusing on the beautiful—whether it was a poem, nature, seeing the horses well and in, or just the pleasure of her own good health. She had an array of emotional tumbling passes that always managed to right her spirit. Rationally, she knew that her father hadn't died on purpose, and she knew her mother did her best to support them, even though she too grieved. But this knowledge did not prevent her from feeling sad and lonely, and she couldn't help fearing to risk her heart that way again. It just seemed to be asking for trouble to start something up with Mark. It would end badly with hurt feelings and then the uncomfortable and inevitable meetings at the farm. "Don't pick your potatoes where you shit, Jane," she could hear her mother bitterly advising.

She did not trust Mark because she didn't trust men in general. As far as she could tell, Mark was perhaps the most baggage-less man she'd ever met. But she was ready to seize upon the only red flag she could discern: that he was forty and, by his own admission, had never had even one "near miss" at a serious relationship. She, at least, had had committed relationships, even though they had not worked out.

Would she marry or was she better off alone? She'd told Abby and Rachel often enough that, while she found the idea of a man attractive in many ways, eventually you also had to accept the inconvenience of their presence—farting, belching, scratching, and consuming all of a woman's natural resources. "I mean," Jane had told Abby recently, "a man is fine to have, but do you really want him hanging around and smelling up the place?"

Perhaps sex without commitment was the best solution—friends with benefits. She certainly did not want anyone to curtail her freedom. She wanted to pursue life on her own terms. Since working at the farm, she was able to send her mother money each month. While she wasn't particularly close to her mother emotionally, she appreciated how hard she'd worked to keep the family together. Her mother still worked, but she was getting on in years now, and Jane was a dutiful, if not a loving daughter.

She needed a free rein to make such decisions. She was sure, despite no evidence, that Mark would not permit the freedom she required. She was so ready to catch that rarified scent of masculine assumption that had been common to her experience of men, she invented it on Mark's behalf. How could it be otherwise? Had patriarchy suddenly died? With all of his money, charm, good looks, and lack of drama, how could he have any real depth? Men, she told herself, expected her wishes, her goals, and dreams to take a back seat to theirs. And when a man accidently shared an idea that she'd already held, he congratulated himself for having thought of it for her. That was how her brothers, her boyfriends, her dissertation advisor, and most of her male colleagues treated women. It was unlikely that Mark could be different, she reasoned. She put the finishing touches on her inner judgment, summing Mark up, "besides, he just wants booty. And I'm not risking my job to be his booty call." Her ire sufficiently aroused by the idea of being remotely sexually used, however unfounded and unfair to Mark, helped Jane tumble past her fear of falling in love and her sadness that a relationship had not, would not work out for her. Anger at the plight of women made her strong. And as the international judges awarded straight tens, she was determined to forget the kiss, and laughed at herself for sequestering it ominously and significantly in "the past."

*

Friday came and Jane was ecstatic when she heard Abby's car roll up the drive. She ran out and greeted her friends and got them thoroughly settled in their rooms. The pair decided that they would be simply snug in Jane's lovely old farmhouse, even if there hadn't been three baths. Jane, of course, still had to do her chores, but Abby and Rachel wanted to help as much as they could, so long as it was afternoon housework and not crack-of-dawn barn work.

Once they were all settled in and Jane had finished her chores with Mac, the girls gathered round the kitchen and prepared their first meal together. Rachel had put a rosemary chicken into the oven. She rubbed the skin with butter and lemon juice, and then dusted it lightly with salt, pepper, and Bell's seasoning. Abby put the finishing touches on an apple pie, and Jane seasoned some small russet potatoes for baking. And they all made contributions to the salad, while they drank wine and chatted freely.

Jane told Abby and Rachel the whole short but intense story of Mark from the beginning, the attraction, the date that was not a date, and that tempestuous kiss that had her knees buckling.

"So, what happened after that?" Abby asked.

"Nothing. He left. Evidently, to go back to the city," Jane said.

Abby asked sympathetically, "Oh, honey, are you okay?"

"Of course! It's not tragic or anything. I'm just a little mixed up about what it is I want or expect. I'm trying not to have expectations—they're the kiss of death, anyway. Besides, I've sworn off men," Jane laughed, pouring herself another glass of wine.

Abby looked hopefully at Rachel and asked if her spidey senses were tingling.

"You know Jane never wants to know her future. She wants to live it, not hear about it. The only strong impression I get is that Jane is...horny," she laughed.

"Rachel! What, horny? Even if I were, he's my boss..."

"True. It's all clear. No conflict except the incredible attraction and the intense desire to damn the torpedoes and away all boats. You know you want to throw caution to the wind and go for it. Fear holds you back." Rachel challenged her.

"Do you think I should? Just let it be light and get crazy with it for as long as it lasts?" Jane asked.

"If you can, why not? The real question is *can* you?" Abby continued, "We all like to think we can be like a guy, have some incredible, frivolous sex, no strings, and then forget about him. But..."

"Yah, I know. It just doesn't work for me," Jane had to admit. "I have to *like* a guy before I can sleep with him, and if the sex is really great—it's like a drug. I'm hooked. And then," she sighed, "somebody's gotta take the three-ten to Yuma. And I love this job, so it ain't gonna be me."

"Relationships are always doomed. It's a wonder the race has survived," Rachel observed. "I read somewhere that there's a chemical released in women's brains when we have sex that produces the feeling of being in L-U-V. I can't remember the name of it, oxytoxy or something, but apparently it's more addictive than crack."

"And yet, part of me wants to go there. Not good." Jane exhaled. "You know how I get. I like a guy, I get infatuated, I get involved, and then…eeeh, scary Jane rises from the grave. Okay, Rachel, I'm ready for my fortune cookie now. Give it to me straight."

"Honestly, Jane, until I've met the man, I can't really say. All guys are dolts when it comes to relationships. He's forty and still single, right? It could go either way—and this is not the psychic talking, just the woman. He might be at a turning point. Maybe he's tired of having any woman he wants and never having to feel responsible. Seriously, some guys change, and some don't."

Jane sighed and Rachel continued, "I know it's hard, but try not to think about him. Just be you."

Chapter Nine

The next day, Jane noticed Mark's Porsche in front of the manor. She ran into him on one of his customary walks as she was coming back from the field with the horses. It had been drizzling and foggy earlier in the morning and was merely gray and damp now. His greeting was warm and friendly. Jane realized that he wasn't about to bring up the fact they'd almost screwed on her kitchen island, and she had no intention of mentioning it. So, they chatted about the farm, and Jane mentioned that her friends were visiting, and that Rachel, her psychic connection, would be happy to play gypsy fortuneteller at the party—"have Ouija, will travel."

She told Mark that she'd taken Rachel and Abby on an abbreviated walking tour of the farm. They'd gone far enough to discover a rather comely old manse that Rachel had particularly admired and was interested in perhaps renting. It needed a lot of attention, but had a wide porch with huge pillars, not unlike the house. Jane couldn't imagine why it was left to rot. It seemed such a grand place rising up from its former lawns, now mere weeds and brush. It was literally molding away.

Continuing with this safe topic, Jane said, "Rachel is quite taken with that *Fall of the House of Usher*-looking mansion—you know, the one about three miles from here. She'd like to rent it, maybe. Do you know the place? It's white, or it was at one time, with green trim. It's a little crazy looking…"

Mark said he'd be glad to let Rachel have the place for free. "But, you should tell her, it's supposedly haunted. No one will stay there for more than a week. My parents tried letting it out for free a bunch of times. No go. We offered it to the crews—guys who eat barbed wire for breakfast, but run like little girls from the old Whitcomb place."

"Haunted?" Jane smiled, "No wonder Rachel likes it—she's a sensitive, you know. She believes in ghosts. What about you? Have you ever stayed there? You know, the requisite twenty-four hours for your inheritance?"

"I don't need an inheritance that bad," he laughed. "No way I've stayed in the place—haunted or not, it's a mess. If your friend is serious, it's hers. I'll see if I can get the crews to work on it—I'll talk to Manuel about it."

"What happened there—who's supposedly haunting the place?"

"That, no one seems to know. An artist lived there a long time ago. That's all I know."

Having exhausted the haunted mansion conversation, and facing another awkward silence, Jane switched the topic to Mac. "Oh, good news: Amazingly, Mac was able to fix the old John Deere. So, we don't need a new one, after all."

"Good for Mac. That saves a tidy sum. Is he still working out?"

"Absolutely! It took him a while to stop calling me 'Miss O'Hara.' He doesn't call me anything, now. He can't seem to wrap his mind around calling me just plain 'Jane.'"

Mark smoothly interjected, "No one could call you 'plain,' Jane."

Jane smiled and blushed. "Well, he's really great with the horses," she said, breezing past the compliment with a smile, "I don't mind saying, I wasn't crazy about handling the stallion, but Mac's got him in hand, beautifully. We should breed our mares this spring and summer. There'll be a new generation of warm-bloods on the farm. By then, the green horses should be well along," She halted abruptly, feeling that she had started to babble. The two horses she had on leads to bring in from the field raised their heads from grazing, their attention diverted by the sound of a car rolling down the gravel road. Relieved from an awkward silence, they saw it was Ben, who waved to them. "Hmm, that's odd. He was just here yesterday to see the stallion," Jane said, perplexed that

Ben was here again so soon. "I'd better go see what he wants." She smiled at Mark and continued toward the barn and Ben.

*

Whew! That's done. And it was fine. Mark sighed, his relief tinged with a slight regret. She really is so lovely. He didn't think he knew any women past thirty who blushed. But Jane did, often. She was such a mysterious combination of competence and shyness, of beauty and lack of self-possession. She was just *interesting*, he thought. When enough distance lay between them, he gave a surreptitious glance over his shoulder. It didn't take Margaret Mead to recognize Date Man. Ben wasn't there for the horses. Mark immediately discerned that Ben was interested in Jane. He was awkwardly holding flowers, for the love of Mike. And he had that slightly spruced-up look with his hair a little slicked back, his clothes less rumpled than his usual country vet appearance. He must have actually run an iron over his khakis, an idea that Mark found mildly annoying because it signaled forethought, planning, effort...*hope*.

And suddenly regret mounted to something like irritation: he was abdicating the field, but ironically resented the idea that someone else might like to picnic there. He had to accept that Jane was a free agent, and if she preferred the likes of Ben to him, well, let her have him, then. He'd already concluded that he had to back off from Jane, for her sake. He wanted her, but it would be selfish of him. Jane just wasn't the "roll in the hay" type. With other women, Mark had always been able to find equal footing. But Jane was different. There was something beguilingly fragile about her, not physically, but he discerned a shyness in her, a depth he couldn't ignore and yet wasn't ready to deal with.

Mark kicked through the grass at his feet, violently smashing a mushroom in his path. He glanced over his shoulder once more, shoved his hands deep into his pockets and picked up speed.

As he imagined Jane being happy with Ben, he acknowledged that Ben was everyone's idea of a good man. "He was the marrying kind, too," he thought. "Hell, even I'd marry Ben." He had a great business, and oozed that boyish folksy charm. Even Mark's mother liked Ben. She'd remarked more than once that Ben was a comfort to have around.

Mark, on the other hand, began to feel a certain inner emptiness. He'd warmed himself by the fires of many women. He never lied to them. But he did withhold truths for which there was no graceful admission. To be perfectly honest, he believed, would have been rude, cruel even, and certainly a mood killer. Sexual intimacy without emotional intimacy was something both men and women craved, wasn't it? Wasn't it perfectly fine to pursue that gratification as long as the woman was consenting and also satisfied—and Mark was very good at that.

He had always believed that it was really women who held all the cards. A man could seduce all he wanted, but a woman got to say "yes" or "no." And his success with women had always seemed ample evidence to support his theories of sexual equality. So he couldn't explain the baffling emotional chaos that often followed a sexual relationship. It seemed that women, whom he'd thought strong and self-assured, became clingy and needy, demanding. He had not considered until that moment that a man's power of seduction capitalized on a woman's hope, especially, if or when she was vulnerable. And why would a woman, he wondered, want to kill a mood by saying, "just so you know, I'm hoping this turns into something." Perhaps, he thought, just as he didn't want to destroy the pleasure of the chase, women didn't want to announce that they hoped to lasso a man.

He began to see that he chose, as if he'd had specially developed radar from NASA, women whom he thought subscribed to his theory of sexual equality, for fun and recreation. He began to understand that there really was no equality between the sexes and wondered if men didn't have an unfair advantage, after all. In fact, he was never attracted to women who approached him, who *really* were on an equal footing with him, who truly wanted only recreational sex. When women pursued him with that assertive, what he regarded an aggressive, interest—no matter how beautiful they were, he was not interested. There was limited pleasure to be had there. He preferred to be the one who "chased" a woman. He enjoyed the seduction far more than the conquest. But once the woman began to have expectations of him, and once he felt that he was disappointing her, he was off and running.

The day was chilly and damp, the sky darkening and gloomy. His pace slowed to a shuffle, and he turned back toward the house with heavy steps. What he needed more than anything this afternoon was a great quantity of Scotch—neat.

Chapter Ten

Ben handed Jane the flowers, the last remaining from his own garden, a wild, rather beautiful arrangement. Jane needed to put them in water, which meant inviting Ben into the house. She liked Ben, and the realization that he was clearly attracted to her pleased her, but didn't necessarily attract her to him in return.

She'd heard enough of the local gossip about Ben to know that he'd been deeply hurt by an ex-wife, and she did not want to lead him on. Still, if he were courageous enough to bring flowers, she would give him a chance to see if he could make her happy. Abby had to be on campus two days each week. It was a school day for her, and Rachel had gone antiquing, so Jane knew the house would be empty. She dismissed immediately the foolish entrance of Mark into her thoughts, as if she were somehow "cheating" on him. "Don't be insane. It was just one kiss," she insisted to herself.

She arranged the flowers with care in a large green-tinted glass vase and chatted amiably with Ben. He was extremely cute. There was no doubt about that. He was tall, but not excessively, measuring in at about five-eleven, she guessed, maybe six feet. She couldn't help mentally sighing at the comparison to Mark's six-three.

Ben had soft brown eyes and sandy colored hair that was beginning to thin in the front. But he had a great build—slender and strong, a winning smile, and he had both a keenness and a kindness about him. He seemed to look deeply into Jane, as if returning her scrutiny. All told, Jane thought he was a great guy with a wonderful career—a career she could enjoy with him and support him in. But, no sizzle, she thought, as she kept her hands around the vase, feeling its round smoothness. "It's too bad my friends are out, Ben, I would have liked introducing you to them," she said. "Would you like a drink?"

"I better not," Ben replied, "I've got to go to Pottersville—a client's hunter colicked last night. I want to make sure that he's okay—the horse, that is."

Jane chuckled. "Colic? What kind?"

"Impaction, most likely. I dosed him with mineral oil, and had the groom keep him moving. He passed stool and seemed okay. I just want to give his barrel a listen."

"We are so lucky to have you as our vet, Ben."

He beamed at her praise, "You do a great job too, Jane. Not many people take temperatures often enough. Say, would you by any chance be interested in going over there with me? I mean, it's not exciting or anything, but if you're interested in colic…"

Sensing Ben's awkwardness, Jane decided to throw him a lifeline. "Sure, I'd love to. I'd like to check out our neighbors' stables."

"Great! Afterwards, if you're hungry, we could get a bite somewhere—have you been to Azzurro's in Peapack yet?"

"No, but I hear it's wonderful. Let me just leave Abby and Rachel a note."

Jane liked that she didn't feel as if she needed to shower and change for Ben. It was just a casual outing, something on the spur of the moment—he probably needed help holding the hunter. And she was actually starving. Italian sounded marvelous.

A few hours later, they were seated at a table for two in the back corner under a window that looked out over a courtyard. The cotton tablecloth was immaculately white offset by the royal blue linens. Ben was appropriately talkative about himself and seemed genuinely interested in Jane, too. She rarely had occasion at the farm to discuss her academic career, though Mark and his parents knew, of course. Still, she'd rarely mentioned that part of her life to Mark, and here was Ben drawing it out of her. He admired her achievement in getting tenure at a major research institution. She found herself growing expansive with him. "I wouldn't cash in for just any job—Nora offered something special. You know how spectacular the farm is, and the house is pretty unbelievable, too. And she pays me more money than God. I'm earning twice what I made as an assistant professor, doing something I love. It's the way of life, you know? I guess what they say about following your bliss is true. But I'm rambling," she laughed.

"Following your bliss is important, so long as a person isn't your bliss," Ben agreed. "I mean, don't you think making other people your happiness is dangerous?" Ben asked.

Jane had the uncomfortable feeling that he was alluding to his former wife. "Yes, I think when we make other people so important, it can backfire. But there are lots of examples where it works out. I mean, look at Nora and Robert Hannon."

"Have you ever loved somebody that way?" he asked.

"Have you?" she coughed evasively, then instantly regretted it. Of course, *he* had.

And the instant she thought it, he said it, "Yep. Sally, my wife."

Jane didn't want to let on that she listened to town gossip, so she asked, "What happened—if you don't mind talking about it?"

"It's a very basic story: I loved her, and she loved me, until one day she didn't anymore. She met somebody and ran off with him."

"I'm sorry, Ben."

"No, it's all right. It hurt like hell for a long time, but I got over it. I hope she's happy, but honestly," he said smiling, "I doubt it. But, she made her choice, and I wish her well. So, what about you? Ever love somebody over the top that way?"

"Maybe once or twice, I thought so." It was actually more like half a dozen times, but who was counting—Jane didn't want to sound like a used up rag of a girl. "I like to think that I learned from my experiences. I don't expect another person to make me happy, and I don't make them responsible for that job."

"What does make you happy, Jane?"

"What I'm doing. I am truly happy working and spending time with the horses and dogs on the farm. I love the people and kids who come for lessons. And, of course, I love my friends, too."

"Don't you want more out of life?"

"What more is there?"

"I dunno. Husband? Kids?"

Jane felt slightly uncomfortable. The conversation was taking a decidedly personal turn. "In theory, sure. It would be nice. But, if I never fall in love or get married and have kids, what I have is pretty wonderful."

"What about your biological clock? Don't most women feel biologically driven to have kids?"

"*Oh my God, check please, he's not going to let up,*" she exclaimed inwardly. "I think it depends on the woman," she said, hoping she didn't appear to be unnaturally cold. "I got a lot of maternal fulfillment from my students, and I get a lot of fulfillment caring for the animals and my friends. I think having a family would be great, but I'm not pining for it. It's okay if it doesn't happen. What about you? Are you champing at the bit to be a daddy?"

Ben chuckled warmly, "Hell yah. I know—I'm a girl," he said as he smiled with some embarrassment. "But not so much that I'd rush into anything with just anyone. I'm actually considering adopting."

"That's great, Ben!"

"Well, I haven't committed to the idea yet, but it's definitely on the table. I mean, I don't think my own DNA is so spectacular that it needs to be re-entered into the gene pool," he laughed modestly.

It was getting late, and they both had to get up very early, but Jane enjoyed her dinner with Ben. He was warm and honest, self-effacing, and…really nice. She didn't tingle in his presence, but she thought he was interesting to know. When he dropped her back at her place, she was punchily sleepy. The eggplant parmesan and the chocolate soufflé she'd had for dessert worked on her like a narcotic. Ben walked her to her door and thanked her for coming out with him. He had his hands shoved deep into his pockets as he looked at her a moment, shyly smiling. Then he put a hand gently on her shoulder and kissed her on the cheek. "Good night, Jane. I'll see you soon," he said, and turned to leave.

As Jane got ready for bed, she thought it was too bad that she felt no zing with Ben, as he was actually quite perfect for her. She decided she wouldn't write him off, however, and was asleep within minutes.

Chapter Eleven

The nine fingers of Jameson he'd had the night before didn't help Mark jump up and greet the morning. He stumbled into the bathroom and threw cold water on his face and the back of his head, and then went back into the bedroom and squinted at the sunny day. He didn't usually overdo it on the drinking.

He saw Jane and another girl, whom he presumed to be a lesson, cantering up the field to the top of the hill with all three dogs in tow, where they turned at the old stone wall. He knew that trail had a fork that went on forever from Bedminster through North Branch and beyond.

The fact that Ben was interested in Jane immediately drove her stock up in Mark's estimation. Whereas he had shuddered at the recent idea that Jane might be more interested in him than he was in her, this morning he felt that if anyone was going to be with her, he wanted it to be him. And yesterday, he'd felt his whole paradigm about women shifting. For the first time in his life, he wondered if it might be possible for him to really love a woman and stick with her. He wondered what it would be like to be that guy who didn't disappoint a woman, who didn't want to get away.

He needed to get to know Jane better to see if his answer lay with her. As he thought of her physically, he decided he needed a nice long shower with lots of slippery sudsing, and a couple of aspirin, too.

Despite twenty minutes under hot water, Mark was still hung over when he descended the stairs. Phillips took one knowing look and said quietly, "Good morning, Mark. You look like you could use a very hearty breakfast," and suggested scrambled eggs, bacon, toast, and coffee. Mark appreciated Phillips' experience. He always knew what to do.

"Have I told you lately that I love you, Phillips?"

"Only with your eyes."

"Don't make me laugh—it hurts."

Mark flopped in the overstuffed chair beside the fireplace in the library and wondered why and when he had decided to drink so much. He checked Bloomberg, and felt his eyes pulse painfully. No numbers today. His iPhone vibrated on the desk. It was Veronica...again. No, he definitely could not deal with Veronica today. Food good, tree pretty—these were the most complex terms he could manage at the moment.

Phillips brought him his breakfast in the library, gently placing the tray on the side table. Mark winced at the small clattering sound of the dishes, Phillips' care notwithstanding. With a commiserating glance at Mark, he left without a word.

After Mark ate and had two cups of coffee, he began to feel more human and determined that a brisk morning walk would restore him completely. Outside, he whistled for the dogs, but then remembered they'd followed Jane out on the trails. She had a way with the dogs. Before she came, they were big and friendly, but oafish and independent. Jane actually had civilized them into respectful creatures. Mark would not have thought Frank capable of learning a command, but Jane had taught him all the basics: come, sit, stay, down, and high five. He had to admit, they were more entertaining to be around.

And he wondered whether she intended to apply her craft with canines to him. Would she have him sitting and staying quietly by her feet, begging in that obscenely cute way that large dogs have, sitting erect on their hindquarters, paws ridiculously dangling in front of them, miserably hopeful and expectant for their liver treat? Would that be Mark in a month, a week? This morning he thought her well worth it, but then, he was so hung over, he was part Basset Hound.

He saw Mac on the tractor out in the distance, spreading manure in the fallow field and decided he'd do some barn chores to help out. He wanted to do something nice for Jane, and he hoped the workout would sweat the hangover from him. Mac or Jane had already turned the horses out and mucked stalls, so he decided to toss down the evening hay, put flakes in the stalls and then empty, clean, and refill all the water buckets. Then he swept the barn, and cleaned out the tack room. He finished raking the outer courtyard of the barn and then surveyed his work with satisfaction. He decided to incorporate barn chores into more of his days, as often as he could.

Putting the barn right and being out in the fresh air helped his head clear. Physical work made him feel clean and whole. He enjoyed his career, too. He liked succeeding, earning, doing, competing. But, his New York life was fast-paced, immediate. Even relationships turned on a dime. He wondered whether he wasn't rather tired of his freedom and superficiality of his pleasure. He thought of Phillips, a relatively poor man, who carried himself like a king. He wondered how much Mary and his kids had to do with that. He thought of Jane. She had a purity about her, to be sure. He smiled as he reflected on her embarrassment at his innuendo at the Tavern, but would have given herself to him in her kitchen, if he'd asked it of her—he was sure. What a curious combination of passion and primness, she was. What a charming set of contradictions. And he was suddenly glad that he hadn't pressed any further.

Mark determined that he would go slow with Jane and would be completely honest with her. "The readiness is all," as Hamlet would say. He wanted to see her again, that's all he knew. He wanted to see if they could start something that might last.

The day was shaping up gorgeously—sunny and crisp, teetering between chilly and warm. He puttered around the barn and kept an eye out for Jane. He decided he'd ask her to go with him for a ride.

He rehearsed his invitation, saying, "Hey, Jane. I thought I'd go for a ride this afternoon and was wondering which horse I should take. And, oh, by the way, would you mind coming with me? I'm afraid..." *Hell no! Afraid? Ugh.* "I thought it would be more prudent..." *Damn. Now he sounded like an English nob,* "not to go out alone in case anything happened, so would you come out with me..." *Yah, the sensible, responsible angle.* "You shouldn't ride or swim alone because you could drown or your horse could get snake bite..." *Oh, shit, no snake bite. Where are we, in the Amazon?*

In the end, Mark determined to keep it simple: "Jane, I'm going out for a ride. Would you mind coming with me?" and congratulated himself on his plan.

When she got back, Mark helped her untack the horses. While she groomed the young Morgan bay, he put the gray thoroughbred away. Nora and Jane knew all the horses' names, but Mark could only go by descriptions: the big chestnut warm-blood, the Morgan bay, the Hanoverian stallion, the Irish draught. He didn't see horses as being personal or having a range of feelings, and therefore didn't associate them with names. He realized that he often thought about women in the same way: the redhead, the blonde, the tall brunette with the long legs. Their names tended to meld into one another's. Except for Jane's. Perhaps because she'd only had a name when his mother first mentioned her. And now each time he saw her, he wanted to say her name, to whisper her name to her.

As they brushed down the horses, he cheerfully called out to her, "Jane, it's a beautiful day for riding the trails, isn't it?"

"Yes, I've just had a great trail ride with Lorie."

You mean the short girl with the light brown hair, Mark thought, but only said, "Oh, Lorie." He paused at the potential derailment of discussing "Lorie" and immediately struck back to his path. "I was thinking of going for a ride myself today..."

But before he could finish his sentence, Jane interrupted, "Really? Your mother said you never ride."

"I used to ride a lot, and I do know how, but I don't go out that often, it's true. Still, it's a great day for a ride." *Let's get back on track.*

"Capital. Lorie and I had a great ride."

"Lorie, yes," he quickly breezed past her, "I was hoping you might like to go out riding with me. It's been a while, and uh, it's safer and more sensible to go with someone rather than alone. Especially since it's been a while since I've ridden…snakes and whatnot," he trailed off, repeating himself.

"Very true. I'd be happy to go. I don't have any lessons scheduled for the afternoon. I have to do a few things at the house, so how does two o'clock sound?"

"Great! Who should I catch? My mother told me the buckskin is great in the field."

"That'd be Jack," Jane said, "yah, he's fabulous and big—you'll look good on him. He's got size and style, but he's a go-pony, whoa-pony at heart. If you want, we can start out in the ring to see how legged up you are."

"I'm legged up just fine," Mark said dryly. "When I bring him in, do you want me to catch a fresh horse for you?"

"I've got Duchess in already—I've been treating her for mud thrush, but she's fine now. She could use a bit of exercise."

"All right then, I'll see you at two."

Chapter Twelve

Jane was fairly flummoxed by Mark's asking her to ride out with him. The torrid kiss she had been trying not to think about was suddenly fresh in her mind. She could still feel his mouth on hers, if she let herself. But she had forbidden herself to think of being attracted to a man who was her boss, not to mention as slippery as mercury. She reflected on the date that was not a date, that ended like a date. And then his leaving, which she interpreted as his avoiding her. If she could just trust herself to have sex with him and take it for what it was, that would solve everything.

She checked her watch. She quickly threw Topsy and Marquessa back into the field, and seeing that Mark had already organized the barn, put Jack and Duchess's tack next to their stalls. That left her with enough time to eat and get ready for the afternoon ride.

She burst through the kitchen door breathlessly, where late-rising Rachel and Abby were making their "morning" coffee, and told them of her afternoon plans. "Rachel, if you've got any of your feelings, tell me now…"

"Wear a jacket; it's gonna get chilly," she smiled.

"Conferring with the spirits of the *Farmers' Almanac*, are we?" Seeing Rachel's eyes darken, she said, "You know something. C'mon, sweetie, don't hold out on me!"

Rachel spoke kindly, "Jane, it's not him that's the problem. It's you, honey. I mean, it's always us that's the problem. You're so attracted to him, you're craving him."

"Isn't that the ironic truth!" Abby asserted, pouring herself a cup coffee. "When we're super attracted, watch out! And the ones we're indifferent about are always hot on our trail."

"It doesn't matter," Jane said, "it's a hopeless situation, anyway."

"Not true, sweetie, there's always hope," Rachel rejoined.

"Oh? Do tell." Abby said on behalf of Jane.

"I don't mean to be cryptic." Rachel exhaled, "You know, being psychic sucks sometimes. Especially the way I do it. The Magic Eight ball says 'try again later.' It's not like I have a roadmap, guys. I can't say anything specific about him—I haven't even met him yet. But I know you, Jane. When you're infatuated, honey, you get a little desperate. If you can, try to let him go a little bit."

Abby, having been through relationship woes with Jane before, said, "Look, whatever happens, we're here for you," and handed Jane a cup of coffee.

Jane sighed, and Rachel added, "Forget the jacket. Bring a blanket—ground's cold this time of year," she laughed and shoved an orange wedge in her mouth.

*

At quarter to two, Jane left the house for the barn (without a blanket) but she did wear a jacket, as the afternoon had turned chilly.

Mark was at the barn when Jane got there and was brushing Jack before tacking him up. Jane went to Duchess's stall and pulled her into the aisle to tack her up. Making conversation, Jane asked Mark when he'd started riding.

"When I was fourteen," he said. "That was quite a while before my parents bought this place. In those days, my mother kept a couple of horses, which she boarded not too far from here, actually. I guess she hoped I would share her love of horses. So she encouraged me to come with her—she bought that place too, eventually. It's part of our property."

"And you fell in love with horses?"

Mark laughed, "Not exactly. I fell in love with Betsy Miller, and Diane Westerly, and Cynthia Buxton, and...well, you get the picture. I was fourteen, and I realized that if you're a guy who likes girls, you can meet a boatload of them in a stable. So, I learned to ride—very well." Amused that Jane overlooked his obvious double entendre, he rescued himself, "I had to outride the girls, didn't I? So, I became fearless over fences. Girls loved it! But I almost broke my neck a couple of times."

"So you don't really care about horses?" Jane asked.

"Oh no, don't get me wrong—horses are great. Beautiful animals," Mark said, "but I've mostly outgrown the riding part of it. Every now and then, though, a trail ride inspires me. I love the outdoors, and seeing it from horseback can be spectacular."

After tacking up, they mounted from the block, and as they walked out, Mark deftly lifted the saddle flap and tightened his girth. Jane did the same. She let Mark take the lead. He was, indeed, legged up. He brought them through paths, fields, woodlands, and over streams, trotting or cantering wherever they could, side by side or single file as needed, and walking when it was all the horses could manage.

Jane declared somewhat nervously, as she looked around, trying to get her bearings, "I've never been this far out. I'm afraid I don't have the greatest sense of direction. I usually stick to trails close to the barn, within a mile or so."

"Ah, but this is so much better. I wonder where we are?" he teased. He took her into rough terrain far off the usual trails and bridle paths. Everything was so beautiful.

After trotting and cantering for a while, they let the horses walk. "I'll probably have to eat off the mantle tomorrow," Mark joked. "So, could you get back on your own if you had to?"

"Uh, the stable's that way?" she smiled, pointing in opposite directions.

"Ah, my plan is working. You'll have to trust me to navigate. I'll be your hero," he said. "Actually, if we keep on this trail," he pointed, "we'll pass out of Bedminster and into North Branch."

Jane looked at the wild brush and tall grasses that surrounded them. "You call this a 'trail'?" she asked.

"Well, it's not a well-worn trail, but yah, this is a trail. There's so much more to see than you can from the trails near the barn," he said excitedly.

"It is breathtaking out here. It's so wild," she smiled, "but let's go slow. I don't want the horses stepping in any gopher holes."

They passed through the tangled brambles and in and out of wooded areas that broke onto more open fields. They rode through these and fluttered birds out of hiding. Jane recalled, "This reminds me of where I grew up—way back off of Route 22 out by Flemington, before so much of it got developed. It was nothing but wilderness and farms when I was a kid. My brothers and I practically lived outdoors. I used to follow my brothers out on their expeditions—they were older and wanted absolutely nothing to do with me. I was really young, and my mother made them take me along. They were supposed to watch out for me."

"Did they?" Mark asked.

"In the indifferent fashion older brothers have—they were pretty young, too. One time, I got tired. We were too far out for them to take me back, and I was too tired to follow them further, so they left me, quite in the wilderness."

"Oh my God. What happened? Obviously, you lived, but were you okay?"

"Yah, I fell asleep in a deer depression. It was pure luck that my bothers found me, on their way back. I never told my mother about that. She would have clobbered my brothers." Jane smiled, "We were poor and in the country. It's a good thing we fell in love with nature—because we had plenty of it—even inside the house. My brothers were always finding things—turtles, lizards, snakes. My brother Jimmy brought home a water moccasin once and let it loose in the house—it was awesome! It's amazing that I survived my childhood," she laughed, "we were pretty feral. Still, it was great, until, my father died. And then," she paused to swallow, "everything changed," and bit the memory off with a smile.

"How old were you then?" Mark asked.

"Ten."

"Oh, so young," Mark winced, "That must've been tough. I'm so sorry."

"It was," she said, appreciating Mark's look of sympathy, but changing the subject, "What about you? Did you have a happy childhood, Mark?"

He laughed, "I would have to be the most ungrateful jerk in the world to say otherwise."

"But?" she asked, leadingly.

Mark paused and continued, "I can't remember the title, but I read this story in college about a man who waited his whole life for a catastrophe he believed would befall him, only it never did. But, in waiting for it, he was afraid to have friends or to get married. He didn't want anyone else to get hurt when the 'thing' happened to him. So, in the end, he never really lived. And, as it turned out, *that* was the catastrophe."

"Ah, yes, Henry James. No one does irony like that! So, do you feel that way—that you're the man to whom nothing happened?"

"Sometimes," he said. "Things were pretty normal for me as a kid—my mother insisted on that. You know, my father got lucky and made his fortune. But my mother wanted me to grow up appreciating stuff, not just expecting things. I went to public school. I actually didn't know just how wealthy my parents were until after law school."

"Really? How did you not know?"

"When I was a kid, we lived a middle-class lifestyle, except for my mother's horses. I had chores and jobs. I worked throughout undergraduate and law school for my own spending money. By that time, I knew my parents were well off—I mean, they paid my tuition, and plenty of people I knew had loans and financial aid.

And then, when I was in law school, they bought Hannon Farm. After I passed the bar, my father asked me to handle the estate, and then I knew just how rich they really were."

"Were you shocked? What did you think?"

"At first, I was shocked. I thought, 'my God, they are millionaires many times over, and I delivered pizzas?!'" he laughed. "But Mom said she wanted me to know what it was like to work and earn my way. I think my parents were so terrified I'd have 'rich-kid, only-child, silver-spoon-up-my-ass syndrome,' that they did everything they could to prevent it. Dad said he was afraid I'd grow up soft and flabby. He was so proud of any sports trophy I won." Mark paused, "I'm sorry, am I blathering?"

"Not at all! You are very different from the few, the very few, really rich kids I ever knew."

"My parents weren't rich, not really. They had a lot of money. There's a difference. I mean, my grandfather owned an auto body shop, and my father worked in it. And Mom was a teacher. That's who they are, and they raised me to compete and earn my way. If they'd let me, I'd take myself out of their will."

"Why would you do that?"

"Because I have my own money, and because my mother once told me that it really bothered her that when she and Dad made me work, I had taken a job from some poor kid who really needed it."

Jane laughed, "*I* was that kid. I used to feel so sorry for myself because I had to work so hard for everything. All of my education was on me. My mother helped as best she could, but she was only a waitress with her own bills to pay. I wish I could hold the view that it was all…character-building."

"But you came out of it great," Mark marveled, "Look at all you've accomplished. You're a genuine scholar. Now *that's* impressive."

"Ugh, scholarship. I hated reading all that dry stuff, and I hated writing my own dry stuff even more. Managing Hannon Farm is a dream come true for me. I feel so alive here."

"Do you ever mind getting up so early every single day?"

"No, not as long as I get to bed early."

"Well," Mark asked with a grin, "what if something…you know…keeps you up at night?"

Jane smiled and urged Duchess on, laughing, "Nothing keeps me up after 10pm!" and cantered ahead.

Mark urged Jack on and caught up with her, and called out—"Head up the hill to the left, I want to show you something."

At the top of the hill, spread out before them was a panoramic view of the Watchungs and fields—a patchwork of green and foliage turned orange, red, yellow, and the deep russet of October. They dismounted and looped the reins loosely about low branches to allow the horses to graze.

"The first time I came upon this view, I wished I could paint," Mark said. "Isn't it gorgeous?"

"Oh, Mark," she said, as if he'd created the scene, himself, "It's beautiful." Jane felt herself standing close to Mark; so close, she could almost feel the backs of their hands touch, and yet not. "It's so lovely," she sighed and felt Mark's hand gently take hers. Surprised and smiling, she looked up at him, hoping he wanted to kiss her. And kiss her, he did. And then, just as in the kitchen, she felt herself mold to his body. He held her steady and secure, as she felt herself warming and relaxing, until her mind stopped its endless chatter. There was the bliss of no thinking, just being. Jane felt Mark's heart beating against her, even through their clothing, as he breathed closely in her ear, softly saying her name, kissing her, and holding her, looking at her with a tender, searching gaze. He filled up her senses with the smells of fall, the sounds of breezes rustling the trees. If he hadn't held her, she believed her knees would have given way. He gently slid his hands underneath her jacket and caressed her back. Jane's yearning nearly brought tears to her eyes. She wanted to fall upon the grass. She was sure she would, and would pull Mark down with her.

But just as Jane was about to sink to the ground, Jack briskly trotted past them. He had obviously loosened himself and was cavorting gaily to his freedom. Jane was the first to notice, and placed her hands on Mark's chest, gently pushing him away from her, arching her back as she did so. "Jack's loose," she rasped. "We have to get him." Jack, determined to be free, trotted further from them when they approached. Jane, on wobbly legs and still breathless, decided she'd have a better chance of catching Jack if she did so from atop Duchess, so she returned and mounted her and rode up to Jack, who finally allowed himself to be caught.

By then, she had cooled sufficiently to be relieved that Jack had prevented her from having wild and passionate sex in the field. *Whoa pony, indeed!* It was romantic where there was true feeling, but seemed crass and vulgar—animal—without it. Her mind clearing, she suggested that they'd better get back. She didn't dare meet Mark's gaze, fearing whatever reaction he might have.

Jane would invite Mark to dinner that very night, if he were free. She needed Rachel to meet him, and hoped that then she could help Jane through her conflicting fear and hope of what might, could, or would be with Mark, whatever it was.

Jane had had her heart broken more than once; and she had broken hearts, too. She had begun lately to give up the hope of an ordinary happiness with a man, such happiness as seemed commonplace for the majority, but that had eluded her. She went to the farm determined to build for herself an alternate happiness, deeply individual to her. It was a mystic kind of awe and joy she felt, as if the very rocks would give up their love to her as she began to know how to ask for it rightly. But the afternoon, riding in the wilds, the air crisp, the sun warm, and Mark—she wondered could that other, simpler happiness also be hers. Could she entrust her happiness to Mark?

Chapter Thirteen

Jane was grateful for Mark's help, putting the barn in order for the night. And as they brought horses in, they continued to chat. Jane asked Mark if he believed he had—what had he called it—"rich-kid, only-child, silver-spoon-up-his-ass" syndrome.

"God, I hope not!" he blurted. "I would have given anything to have siblings. When I was really little, I used to ask my mother for a brother or a sister on my birthdays and at Christmas," he said thoughtfully, "and then, after a while, I stopped asking. I could see it tore my mother up. They had me in every club, every team, boy scouts, eagle scouts, the works, to make sure I bounced off of other kids."

"Did they consider adopting?" Jane asked.

"I never asked, but I think they assumed that they were going to have more children of their own. And then, later, Hannon Farm was Mom's way of surrounding herself with kids. I'll tell you one thing, Jane, I would never want to have just one kid. I'd rather adopt a dozen."

*

By the time they finished setting the barn right, it was nearly six. "I'm starved," Jane said, "would you like to have dinner with me and my friends?" Mark was intrigued at the prospect of meeting Jane's friends. It felt rather as though he were being invited "home to meet the family," a relationship milestone that suggested a step further toward deepening their connection—and he was starving, too.

They entered the house through the kitchen, where Rachel and Abby were in the middle of preparing dinner. Jane introduced Mark, and Abby said, "Hi, Jane's told us so much about you."

"Nothing bad, I hope," Mark smiled as he shook hands.

"Oh, no! It's all good," Abby assured him.

Rachel was roughly chopping an onion, while she gave Mark a smiling appraisal. "Absolutely!" she echoed. "Jane tells us you're a lawyer and an investor. Sounds exciting."

"And, he's good in the kitchen—I've seen him slice carrots myself," Jane added as she took Mark's jacket for him.

"My mamma didn't raise no slackers. What can I do to help?"

Abby said, "We're making a stew," and passed Mark some potatoes and a peeler.

"How about a glass of wine?" Jane offered.

"That would be perfect, thanks."

Jane got two glasses from the cabinet and poured the wine from the mag on the counter. "Hmmm, rare vintage—did you bust the piggy bank?" she asked Abby.

"I have the palate of a retriever. So long as I can lap it up, I'm happy," Abby said, adding, "Frank agrees with me, right boy?" Frank, watching the group from his corner in the kitchen, pricked his ears.

"Tell me you didn't give wine to my dog," Jane admonished.

"Silly child. Of course not," Abby reassured her.

"Frank's a beer dog anyway," Mark said as tossed a peeled potato into the colander for rinsing.

"So Rachel, I meant to thank you for agreeing to be our gypsy fortuneteller," Mark said.

"No problem, I'm hoping to get some clients out of it, so it works for me."

"The locals will be talking about it for weeks, I'm sure. We're very provincial here. So how do you do it?" Mark asked.

Rachel asked, "Do what? Oh! Give psychic readings. Would you like a demonstration?" shooting a glance at Jane.

"Absolutely!" Mark said, "I want to make sure my guests will be happy."

Rachel looked at him a moment and said, "Okay, let me tell you how I work. First of all, I don't know any other psychics—ironic, I know. So I'm not sure whether they use Ouija boards or Magic Eight balls or divining rods. Personally, I don't like cliché paranormal objects, so what I usually do is draw."

"Jane mentioned that, and that you also sell the artwork to clients."

"Yes, if they want it, which sometimes they do. I mean, it's a direct reflection of them. Trust me: I'm not getting rich on either the readings or the art." She paused to scrape the onions into the pot and rinsed her hands before continuing. "So here's what I do: First, I have an ironclad rule never to tell anyone any bad things. Not that I've ever seen anything really bad—I'm pretty sure my subconscious mind blocks me. It's too much responsibility. When I see potentially bad things, I try to see the solution."

"Can you see the next Triple Crown by any chance?" Mark joked.

"Eh, no. Sorry. Also," Rachel continued, "my 'awareness' or 'insight' or whatever you want to call it is not based on any direct vision. I mean, it's not as if I'm watching TV and describing the show. It's a lot vaguer, as Jane can attest from experience—more impressionistic and peripheral. That's why I draw. I need a direct object to focus on, and while I'm drawing, the peripheral information sort of comes to me. It's all very inexact, I'm afraid. But that's basically how it works. The whole thing is incredibly imperfect, but I am getting better at it or, trying to, anyway. Oh," she added as an afterthought, "oddly, while details are usually muddled, I often get names or close approximations. I don't know why."

While Rachel explained her methods, Jane slipped out and returned with some paper and a number two pencil, and placed them in front of Rachel.

"Are you ready?" Rachel asked Mark.

"I'm all set. Be gentle, it's my first time," he laughed nervously.

"Double, double toil and trouble; Fire burn, and cauldron bubble," Rachel crackled in a fake spooky voice. And seeing Mark's momentary alarm, she laughed, "I'm kidding, silly."

"Those Shakespeare lessons will come in handy, Mark," Jane quipped.

"I do know Macbeth...that part anyway. A little sensitivity here, please. I'm a fortune virgin."

"Shhhhh," Rachel ordered, "I can't hear the witches, I mean myself, think."

As they settled down, Rachel began sketching. After a short silence, she smiled and said, "I see an older woman, she's very beautiful. She has sparkling green eyes and a dimple on the left side of her mouth. She's Celtic looking—Irish or Scottish. She could be a warrior, but she prefers the hearth. Mona...Lora...no, that's not right..."

"Nora. She's my mother." Incredulous, he turned to Jane. "You told Rachel about my mother, didn't you?"

"Of course. I told Rachel all about your mother and her dimple, and how everyone thinks 'Celtic Warrior' when they see her," Jane laughed, "I mean, she gets that a lot, right?"

Rachel shushed them again and as she continued drawing, she remarked, "She's very happy. She loves you for all that you've done for her. She's so proud of you. She's beaming."

"That's nice. What did I do that's made her so happy, so I'll be sure to follow through when the time comes."

"You gave her her heart's desire."

"Grandchildren. It's gotta be grandchildren. Good to know I have it in me," Mark said, not for an instant believing that Rachel could see anything about his future. He glanced at Jane and smiled.

"I'm seeing another very different woman," Rachel continued. "Young. Good Lord, she's larger than life. Dark. Her hair is long and black, and her face is a ghastly white. She's pointing at you, accusing you. She's leaning over her stove, but she's not cooking anything. Now she's in the center of a beautiful room. People are watching her. We're watching her. We can't take our eyes off of her…" Suddenly, Rachel gasped, "Look out!" and ducked her head.

Jane and Abby started and gave each other surprised looks—they'd never seen Rachel so involved in a reading before. With them, her readings were always sort of wishy washy and vague. This reading was more detailed and a little weird.

"What happened?" Mark asked.

"Sorry. Nothing, really. The dark-haired woman struck a fist, and when she opened her fist, a black bird flew out of it. It surprised me, that's all," Rachel said. "Like that Luis Bunuel film, where a guy opens his hand, and ants are crawling in it."

Mark looked from Abby to Jane, an eyebrow cocked.

"The dark woman, looks kind of like Morticia from the *Addam's Family*," Rachel continued, "only not cuddly like Morticia. She's angry and surreal. She's mad at you, Mark. Victoria…or… Valencia…no…it's Veronica."

"Okay, then, let's everybody calm down." Mark jittered more to himself than the others. "Rachel, now you're scaring me. You read about Veronica in the tabloids, yah?" he asked.

Rachel looked up at Mark as the darkness in her eyes lifted, and her pupils returned to normal. She looked at her drawing and folded the paper in half. "Sorry, Mark. Tabloids are Abby's weakness." Rachel shivered. "Veronica makes quite an impression."

"No, it's okay, I know she's pissed. One thing's for sure, you're the real deal," Mark said, shifting the conversation.

"Do you care to discuss Veronica troubles with us girls?" Abby cheerfully chimed in.

"Hmm, not this time, thanks," he said, glancing at Jane.

Mark helped set the table, and they all chatted casually. Rachel herself became more cheerily animated than usual, as if she more than anyone wanted to put the psychic episode behind her. Jane brought the stew to the table. They all ate and drank liberally and were very congenial in their conversation.

Mark enjoyed Jane's friends as if he were among the sisters of his girlfriend. He didn't cast it in those words, but there was a definitely pleasant familial feeling and comfort in being accepted in their company. He hadn't had much exposure to women as friends, just the odd wife of a business friend, like Phoebe. And he was surprised that he'd enjoyed himself so much. For the first time, he understood the power of female friendship freely offered, and he found himself really hoping that they liked him.

Chapter Fourteen

Jane saw Mark to the door and they said good night. He thanked her for dinner. After their passion on the trail ride, he seemed a little distant, withdrawn. Instead of a kiss, he gave her a brief, rather official hug and said that he'd call her. Jane, disillusioned so many times over the promised call from a man that never came, decided she would not hold her breath. She had just about made up her mind that she would give her all to building something with Mark, and he was suddenly remote. As she closed the door behind Mark, she sagged against it, momentarily drained. She went back to the kitchen and picked up the drawing Rachel had folded. In her hands, she held a drawing of a little girl, sleeping in tall grass.

"Rachel, what do make of this?" she was curious to know.

"You tell me, Jane," she replied. "It was hard to get anything straight. I was inundated with feelings—starting by the way, with very strong make-out images. Oh, yah, I had no idea you were such a nature girl." she said laughing.

"Aieee," Jane cringed, "That's mortifying."

"Hey, girl's gotta get her kicks somehow." Rachel pointed to the picture she'd drawn, "It's you, isn't it?"

"Yes, but why? What does this mean?"

"It came from Mark—it's a picture he had of you in his head," Rachel proposed, and Abby agreed, "Why don't you tell us how things went this afternoon, and maybe we can help you figure it out."

"Well," Jane began, "First of all, I really think I've misjudged Mark in my head. I've been assuming he just wants casual sex, and that he's selfish and spoiled, and a chauvinist. (Jeez, I've got issues). But on the trail ride today, he was so incredibly nice. He was so real, you know? He was honest and forthcoming, like he really wanted me to know who he is. I felt so connected to him." Jane shook her head and recounted all the things they'd talked about and how she'd shared with him a memory about when she was little and her brothers left her sleeping in a deer depression—just as in Rachel's drawing—and that she'd told him about her father dying not long after that when she was ten, and how she didn't want to make a big deal about it. And then she told them about their kissing (again) and how she wanted so badly to let caution fly, but was later relieved that she'd been prevented by Jack's getting loose.

"Ach," Jane exhaled, "but it's not sex that bothers me—that I'm good with—well, as good as a formally catechized Catholic girl can be. It's what happens after—the letdown. You know how when you dream and forget the dream, but during the day something happens or somebody says something, and suddenly the dream rushes back? The instant I saw the drawing, I remembered how when I was a kid, after my father died…oh, you can't imagine how it felt. He was *everything* to me. I think I've always been so afraid to love that hard again. And now here's Mark, and there's me," she gestured diffidently to the picture Rachel had drawn. "It's scary to want someone that much."

"Don't be so hard on yourself, kiddo," Abby consoled her, "I think sometimes men come along to show us what's going on inside. In that sense, Mark is your knight in shiny bright armor. He's bringing you this insight about yourself—right, Rachel?"

"Absolutely," Rachel soothed. "You're not that little girl anymore, sweetie. It's time to start a new story of you. What do you tell your riding students when they're afraid?"

"I tell them not to be, because they're conquering their fear by being on the horse," she said. "I've always had to be so strong. I had to swallow my feelings as a kid. My mother was on lockdown. I was a mess, she was a mess, the whole situation was a mess. There just wasn't anywhere to turn."

"There you go, Jane," Abby consoled, "it's time to let the old wound air out and heal. It's like you fell off the horse, and you have to get back on. Or make your peace with who you are. Accept yourself and the limitations that only you impose."

"I'm just so tired of being taken on a test drive, hired for a job on probation, tried out for the minors. I'm thirty-five years old. I ain't gettin' any younger," Jane sighed. "It would just hurt so bad if I let myself love Mark only to find I'd made another howling mistake."

"Whatever it is, sweetie, you're already in it. Stop trying to control everything and give him a chance. Look, if he's a jerk, you'll live—you know you will, you have before. And if he's not a jerk, well, that'd be pretty cool, wouldn't it? You know the river flows, you don't have to push it," Rachel advised.

Jane inhaled suddenly and sighed. "Just when I think I'm over all of my issues, the riverbed gets stirred up, and the waters are murky all over again."

Jane had been staring off in the distance, when Rachel intruded, "What are you thinking, sweetie?"

"About my mother," Jane sighed. "She loves me, I know that. But it isn't a warm mother/daughter thing. I missed out on that. I'm pissed that she couldn't do any more than she did, and I feel guilty because I couldn't either. I adored my father, but the daddy/daughter thing died with him. When I first read Shakespeare, I was actually jealous of Hamlet—at least he got to chitchat with his father, even if he was a ghost."

Jane thought of the Henry James story that Mark had remembered. Truly, it was a great mistake, the greatest of all, to avoid living for fear of pain.

*

After Mark left Jane's, he was exhausted. It had been a long day out of doors that had begun with a hangover, and he was drained. He went to the library, checked email, and collapsed into the chair by the fireplace. Phillips was checking the downstairs before retiring, and Mark asked him if he'd have a drink with him.

As he handed Phillips a Scotch, he said, "Phillips, you've known me since I was a kid. You're one of the few people in this world whose opinion really matters to me."

"Oh well, you've always been a brat, Mark, if that helps," Phillips laughed as he sipped his drink, "but," knowing the quality of Mark's Scotch, "a generous one." And then seeing Mark's serious expression, he said, "What's going on? Why so serious?"

"I don't know. It's just that I feel as though I've lived so selfishly. I've never had to conquer anything. I've never had to struggle… I've never committed to anyone, not really." Looking at Phillips, he said, "I envy you. Did you know that? You, Mary, and the kids. You've really got it all. I think I'm seeing that more clearly than I ever did before."

Phillips tossed back his Scotch and set his glass down. He had envied Mark's freedom, privileges, and entitlements often during the years he'd been in service with the Hannons. Oh, they were good people, to be sure, and Mark was almost like a little brother. "You're a decent enough chap, Mark. You could have turned out a real prick, if you were selfish. But you're not. You know that."

Switching a gear, Mark asked, "What do you think of Jane?"

"Jane? She's great. But you should be careful, Mark. No offense, but you've tended to trifle with women, and Mary will rip your heart out if you hurt Jane. They're getting pretty tight."

"Going carefully is the problem," Mark sighed. "I want to go slow. But every time I'm with her, slow goes out the window."

"Mary and I had the same problem," Phillips laughed, "and look at us. Oh, sex is exciting, especially in the beginning. But, if you want to have something real, Mark, you've got to decide and then stick to that decision, no matter what. And when you do… when you have that kind of love…it makes a man out of you,"

Phillips smiled and rose. "Okay, speaking of being a man, we've bonded enough. I need to get home to my wife."

When Mark was alone again, he thought about what Phillips had said. Mark considered the last twenty years of his life and suddenly felt hollow. We are not stuck with what fate gives us. We make ourselves by choosing. He raised his glass in silent toast, "to Phillips" and coiffed it.

Chapter Fifteen

The entire county was abuzz with the Dragon's Ball just a few days away. Hannon parties were always exceptional. The Hannon property was so vast that the "locals" consisted of several village centers in Oldwick, Tewkesbury, Peapack-Gladstone, Far Hills, Bedminster, and Bernardsville of all economic strata. The area of Bedminster in particular, where unimaginably wealthy people had lived for generations—the lockjaws, as they were known even among themselves, but especially to those who merely earned money—anticipated the event with particular eagerness.

Jane was just letting the two-year-old colts out after their training session, which consisted of round penning them and getting them to look at her, then reverse directions by turning in toward her. With each little training session, these colts had built up their ability to communicate with Jane and to accept her leadership. Mac had been showing her how to handle them properly. "It's better to train them together at first. Then, cut one away and work him while they're both in the pen. That's the first stage in separating them from each other. Next week, you'll work them one at a time, with the buddy tied outside the pen, and the week after, you'll increase the distance more, until you finally have them weaned off each other. Do it slow like that, and they won't get traumatized." Mac knew how horses think, and his advice was indispensable.

She was just turning them out to the field when she saw Nora and Robert driving down the gravel road to the stable. She couldn't have been more eager to see them than if they had been her own parents. Sometimes she secretly and guiltily pretended Nora and Robert were her parents.

"Mr. and Mrs. Hannon! How good to see you both again," she said smiling radiantly.

"Robert, do you hear this insolent girl? Whatever happened to 'Nora' and 'Robert' and hugs all around?" Nora said, as she kissed Jane warmly and told her, "I've missed you, Jane, and this place," she said, surveying the immediate grounds. "Is everything going well?"

"Yes, but what brings you back? I thought you were up to your eyeballs sorting out the new farm," said Jane.

"The party of course!" Robert asserted. "We got the invitation to the Dragon's Ball and wanted to get here just a bit early."

"Robert, let's find that son of ours and have him help with the bags. Phillips too. Oh, I've missed this place, Jane," she chattered, linking arms with her. "There will never be another Hannon farm like this one. This was the first. Can you come to the house for lunch? Have you eaten?"

"I'm always hungry. The farm has me stoking at least 3,000 calories a day—I'd be a blimp if it wasn't for the work!"

"Well, let's go in and eat then. Phillips is expecting us—I called him last night. But I wanted to surprise Mark."

As they entered the house, Jane commented, "You must have missed Mark—that's the real reason you came back."

Robert heartily rejoined, "Hell, no! We came back for the party. Nora can't resist a costume ball," and then demurred, "But I refuse to dress up."

Nora flung Robert a glance and said, "Robert, we'll find you some suitably masculine costume, don't worry, dear." And to Jane she said, "Of course we missed Mark, dear. Has he been behaving himself?"

Jane could not help but color and said awkwardly, "Perfectly, er, I hope you'll like the decorations, Nora. Tonight we'll light the place up—the decorators just finished yesterday. It's like Halloween fairy land at night."

"Oh, I can't wait. Halloween and Christmas are my favorite holidays. By the way, Mark told us last week that he'd arranged for a psychic through your circle of friends. I'm looking forward to meeting her. Mark said she's got just the right eerie quality."

"Yes, she's definitely got the gift, Nora. Did Mark tell you she had a vision of you? She has seen you brimming with happiness," Jane was delighted to report.

"Well then. She must be good and *completely* authentic." As they entered the house, Mark met them at the door, hugged his mother, shook hands with his father, and smiled warmly at Jane. Holding his mother at arm's length he asked, "Has Jane filled you in on all the details about the party? She's the idea person on this one, Mom."

"So long as there's plenty of food and drink, I daresay everyone will be happy," Nora chimed in.

"Especially drink," Robert added. "You cannot have a good party without free flowing wine."

"Oh, Robert," Nora scolded, "you'll have Jane thinking we're a bunch of alcoholics," and linking arms with Jane, "by the way, I have a 64-year-old bottle of McAllan I've been saving, Jane—do you like Scotch?"

"Me? Scotch? I might be in danger of public singing and dancing, so I better limit myself to one," Jane laughed.

"Oh, I don't know, Jane," Mark offered, "I think seeing you out of control would be very interesting."

*

Robert had been wanting to replace the p-traps in their bathroom sinks for some time. And after lunch, he knew Nora would be busy making phone calls and catching up on her correspondence and decided it would be the perfect time. He didn't have to fix p-traps or tinker with the car for that matter. But he liked fixing and tinkering and getting his hands dirty, even though Nora hated him to.

He spread his towel on the floor. He thought of using Nora's as well for extra cushioning, but after more than forty years of marriage, he could hear the hoop and holler that would cause, *"Oh Rob! Not my good organic cotton bath towels!" You'd think they were woven from unicorn fur,* he mused. He said a quick prayer that God would bless Nora and keep her out of the bathroom until he was finished. He'd clean everything up and wash the towel himself. Nora would never know.

As he mused pleasantly about a job to do, Robert switched from being on his knees to sitting cross legged, reaching under the sink with the pipe wrench to loosen the collar bolts on the old p-trap. He'd do Nora's first, since hers was running slowest. That's what had signaled him to look at the p-traps in the first place. *She's got a mess a hair,* he thought gratefully that his wife's hair and looks had generally held up well, *and a great figure still. Oh, she's got a sag or two, but who doesn't at our age?* he thought, pulling the newspaper nearby so he could dump the trap onto it if he needed to. Robert assured Nora, who hated messes, that a professional plumber would make more of a mess than he would. For some reason, unaccountable to him, Nora could tolerate a stranger's mess better than she could his. *I'll never understand Nora completely,* he thought. Robert was determined to be as careful as he knew Nora would have liked had she been standing over his shoulder. *And thank God, she ain't.*

The collar bolt wasn't loosening up easily, and Robert suspected it was soldered on. He tightened the pipe wrench and began to apply more pressure. He didn't want to bust the sleeves. He thought it was just beginning to loosen, when Nora exploded into the bedroom, shouting, "Robert? Robert! Where are you? Are you here?"

"Yes, Nora, I'm in the bathroom," he blurted, cringing with expectation of the tongue lashing he was about to receive. "What

is it?" he piped from underneath the sink. "Is everything all right...
dear?" (adding the dear defensively at the last second).

"Yes, at least I think so," and seeing Rob squatting like an
Indian, Nora sighed, "oh Robert, not my good organic towels..."
Robert aggressively failed to hear her, so long practiced was he
at ignoring certain intonations of his wife, especially when he'd
already elected an irreversible action. Still, her disapproval was like
acid on his skin. But she was too excited about her news to linger
over the towels for long in any event.

"Robert, did you notice anything unusual about Mark at
lunch?"

"Unusual?" he inquired, still twisting at the collar bolt with his
hand, "where's my wrench?" he muttered to himself, "I just had it
a second ago..."

"Robert!" she said, noticing the wrench's form beneath the
towel, fetched it out, and passed it to him. Robert would have
looked about him for ten minutes before thinking to lift the towel.

"Well, dear, did you notice anything at lunch?" Exasperated, she
continued, "Mark could hardly take his eyes off of Jane throughout
the whole of lunch, dear. I think they might be serious."

Robert bumped his head, turning to look at Nora. "Ouch!"
he said, rubbing his head, "You don't say?" As the smart left, he
looked at his wife, marveling at her and not for the first time in
their long marriage. "How do you *know* these things, love? Are you
part satellite dish or something?" he asked returning his attention
to the sink. "So, tell me everything!"

Nora plunked down on the bathroom floor and told Robert all
that she observed.

*

Jane worked off the rich Beef Wellington and Nora's generous pour
of McAllan with the afternoon barn chores. After her three p.m.

lesson, she decided to work Dividend, a beautiful gray Irish Draught/ Thoroughbred cross that Nora had acquired for Mark. Mark named him but had done little else with him, so at five years, the horse was still green. He was a large-boned, heavy hunter, standing seventeen hands, and had the personality of a kitten. He needed only exposure to educate him, and Jane had been taking him out in the fields and down to Lamington Road to accustom him to traffic. At the farm, she and Mac had him walking over mattresses and tarps, tires, and anything she could find that initially caused Dividend to blow cautiously through his nostrils, but then settle down and accept what she presented to him.

Her goal was to make him bombproof. Dividend did not spook easily—he was generally calm in his nature. But Jane saw an opportunity to make him into a wise horse—a horse that knew how to master his own fear when it arose. That kind of horse was not an easy find. And with his good looks, size, and innate gentleness, adding courage would make him priceless. Jane had high hopes of seeing this horse in Olympic competition one day.

As she walked him out after his training back to the barn, she saw Ben waiting at the entrance. *Och, at least he doesn't have flowers*, Jane observed with relief.

"Hey, Ben, did I forget something?" she asked. "I wasn't expecting you today."

Ben toed his foot in the gravel and shoved his hands deep into his pockets, and said with chagrin, "I came to ask your advice about this masquerade party."

"Don't tell me," she said. "You don't want to dress up. What is it with you guys? None of you wants to dress up for Halloween."

"Geez, Jane, it's not very…manly," Ben stammered awkwardly.

"But it will be so much fun, Ben. So, you need help with a costume?"

"If you wouldn't mind. I don't want to look ridiculous. And nothing too showy—absolutely no leotards."

"I guess Grape from the Fruit-of-the-Loom is out, then," Jane laughed.

She removed the tack from Dividend and checked his chest for heat. Satisfied that he was completely cool, she put him in his stall and threw him some hay and checked his water bucket. She would turn him out later. "Let's go to the house and consult with the experts," Jane offered, "Abby and Rachel are better at this sort of thing than I am."

"But aren't you dressing up?" Ben asked.

"Yes, but Mark is having his friend, Phoebe, fix us up. She's a designer and stylist who makes costumes on Broadway. So, I don't have to be creative at all. Matter of fact, I'm not sure what I'm going as myself, yet." As they walked toward Jane's house, the dogs roused themselves to follow. They nosed at Jane's hands briefly, and she made them stay on the porch off the kitchen.

Rachel and Abby were watching TV in the den, when Jane called out, "Rachel, Abby, come meet Ben!"

Rachel and Abby scurried to the kitchen where Jane presented them. "Ben, these are my best friends, Rachel and Abby," and gesturing toward Ben, "Ben is our farm veterinarian, but for your purposes, he's a guy who needs a Halloween costume."

Rachel and Abby sized him up, turned him around, took his cap off his head, and muttered and conferred with each other. They finally settled on John Wayne as The Quiet Man, although Ben didn't think anyone would get the reference.

"It is a reach," Abby agreed. "But, if we Irish you up too much, people will be asking you where the lucky charms are."

Jane suggested Ben stay for dinner, if he liked, and began rummaging through the fridge. "Ben, do you like meatloaf? Abby makes the very best meatloaf ever."

"Yes, it's a simple dish," she averred, "but I make it well—it's all in the onions."

"C'mon, Abby, you know you've got a few secret ingredients," Rachel said more to Ben than to Abby.

"Do tell, Miss Abby, my bachelor's cooking could use a good simple recipe," Ben said.

"Well, it's the spices—fennel, turmeric, and cumin, onions, and—don't laugh—cranberries. Sometimes I chop green olives in there as well."

"Yah, all's fair in love and meatloaf, I hear." Jane said, smiling toward Abby. "Would you like some wine, Ben? I happened to have picked up a very nice Merlot."

Jane observed Ben and her friends in easy conversation and took the opportunity to reappraise him. She wondered if that kind of spontaneous sizzle she felt for Mark could be manufactured over time for Ben. He was, after all, so appropriate for her, and he fit in well with her friends. He had such easy-going and unassuming manners. Like Mark, Ben was a man she could be proud of. And, perhaps Ben had the greater claim as his living directly eased suffering. Mark's generous charity work, though, had the broader impact. As she observed Abby interacting with Ben, she saw her friend's eyes widen ever so slightly, her color rise, and when Abby laughed…well, Jane knew that laugh. Abby was clearly interested in Ben, and Jane found that she did not mind in the least.

*

Jane excused herself from her company for a few minutes to check horses for the night. "I'll be back in a minute," she said, throwing her jacket on, "I just want to shut the barn up for the night." As she walked the short distance from her house to the barn, she ran into Mark, out for an evening constitutional, who offered to check the barn with her and close it up for the night.

"We're just about to have dinner, Mark, would you like to join us?" she offered.

"Ordinarily, I would love to, but Dad's expecting me to go over some documents with him tonight."

As they entered the barn, they heard the dreadful sounds of a cast horse, stuck in its stall and thrashing to get up. Horses infrequently get cast, but it is traumatizing to observe them panicking and kicking as they try to right themselves. Sometimes, a cast horse will injure itself badly. And Jane panicked at the sound of a struggling horse. She'd only seen a few cast horses when she was young, and only knew they were dangerous to even try to help, especially if you didn't know what you were about.

As they jogged the aisle to find which of the horses had gotten cast, Jane was particularly upset to find that it was Dividend. Mark immediately flung the stall door open and did the only right thing one could do in that situation. He grabbed a wad of mane at Dividend's poll and pulled his head back. Jane followed Mark into the stall, and Dividend, well acquainted with her voice, calmed down, allowing himself to be dragged off the wall inch by inch. Once they sufficiently angled him, they got out of his way so he could right himself and stand. Crisis averted.

"Thank you, Mark," Jane exhaled with relief. "I have never really known what to do with a cast horse—I've seen people get hurt before trying to help."

"The trick is to stay at their head, out of the way of flailing hooves. And, of course, you have to stay calm or it just makes the horse panic more."

"You're actually quite a horseman, Mark. I'm impressed."

"I told you, I have mad skills with horses," he laughed, "—always have. Let's just take him out and walk him up the aisle—just to be sure he's not lame."

Mark walked Dividend up and down the aisle for Jane, who ran her hand over the horse's legs to be reassured he had not injured himself. As they put him away, Mark took the opportunity to say, "Jane, I'm so glad you came to the farm. Are you happy here?"

"Incredibly, Mark."

"I don't want to complicate things, but I want to get to know you better. I want to spend time with you, Jane."

Jane was about to melt and give her assent to Mark when Ben appeared, "Hi—I just came out to see if you were okay—Abby says dinner's ready."

"Oh, Ben, yes, one of the horses got cast. Thank God, Mark was here. I'll be right in, thanks."

As Ben left, Jane turned to Mark, "I'm not going to lie, Mark—I am attracted to you, too—a lot. But it does complicate things here for me. Can we take it slow?"

Chapter Sixteen

With the party just a day away, Phoebe was busy at Hannon Farm ensuring Mark, Jane and Mark's parents were comfortably and stylishly costumed. They were in Mark's bedroom suite, which consisted of a large sleeping area, which opened to an equally large sitting-office area, with a bar at one end, and a large dressing room and bath at the other.

Phoebe sighed, "Honestly, Mark, you're impossible. Why do you even pretend to wear a costume? Why don't you just pull a random gray suit out of your closet and go as a stuffy investment lawyer?"

"Now that's a costume I've never seen him wear," remarked Jane.

"I just don't want to dress like a Renaissance fair guy—absolutely no leotards. I know you brought me something masculine and not too ostentatious, Phoebe, so let's see it."

"Funny, your father said the same thing when I suggested Robin Hood to him. 'No tights!' Well, I could put your father in a gray suit and you in a tuxedo—you could be Q and Bond."

"Bond, James Bond." Mark recited, "I like it. And I have a tuxedo that fits, I think. And Jane, you could be Pussy Galore," he said just to watch her blush.

At that suggestion, Jane emitted a sound—something between a cough, a laugh, and a snort. Had it extended beyond a second, Mark would have dialed 911.

"Right," Mark said, "well, how about Dracula? I'm sure the black cape is iconic enough. Do you happen to have one in your trunk, Phoebe?"

"As a matter of fact, I do—it's from the *Phantom of the Opera*—and it's exquisitely tailored with a deep red lining. A little makeup and badaboom!" Phoebe hauled out the cape and tossed it around his shoulders. "Perfect," she said. "Black pants, white shirt, a little food coloring on the collar, and you're all set. Zinc oxide and rouge optional."

"Very optional," Mark countered. "So what did you pull together for my parents?"

"Your dad is going to be dressed as Sherlock Holmes or perhaps Henry Higgins—it's basically the same look. I'm leaning toward Henry Higgins because your mother refuses to be Watson, but likes the idea of being Eliza Doolittle. She's trying on costumes, now." Phoebe turned to Jane and said, "So, Jane, how do you see yourself this Halloween?"

"In anything but boots and britches or khakis."

"I think I've got just the thing," she said, rummaging through her trunk of costumes, "very sophisticated, designed by master couturier Donatella Versace, and knocked off by Target." She pulled out an exquisite strapless maroon silk dress with a broad slit that went up the side and continued in a curve across the back. "It's half a dress, really, held in place by seamless beige mesh," Phoebe continued, "I hope you know, Jane, not just anyone can wear this costume, but it'll look fabulous on you—you don't have an ounce of fat."

"Uh..." Jane stammered, "it looks like a sock. Where's the dress?"

"It's stretchy and ultra sexy, but it's carefully cut and structured to conceal all the vitals, and it's got these clever clasps to release it," Phoebe reassured her. "Try it on. It's gonna look great, and for modesty purposes, you can toss this black mesh drape over it. It teases the eye."

"To what, fall out of the socket?" Mark laughed, "C'mon, give it a whirl, Jane. You're among friends."

"You can be Mark's lady vampire friend—Contessa De Muerte, Queen of the Damned. The color actually matches the lining of the cape. Here ya go," Phoebe said, handing her the ensemble.

Jane took the costume, more a hint of a dress than an actual garment, into Mark's dressing room to try it on. Unclasped, it was surprisingly easy to slip into. It was also surprisingly comfortable, but then she remembered that these were not ordinary costumes, but professionally made costumes for the stage. She supposed they had to be somewhat comfortable for the actors to move in.

Jane was not a snoop, but she couldn't help looking around Mark's huge bath—adjacent to the dressing room that boasted an entire wall of mirrors. She wondered if Mark had made that design call, and quickly shredded the idea. *Must have been Nora.* The countertops were a dark chocolate-flecked granite, the twin sinks were large sunken stainless steel bowls. The walls were a burnt umber, and the tiling a natural warm beige. But for the dressy wall of mirrors, it was very masculine.

Jane maneuvered the skin-tight dress around, ensuring that the beige path didn't reveal her forensic evidence. The miracle of spandex gave enough to fit snuggly, sans muffining. But there was no way she'd take off the mesh overtop.

She shyly re-entered the bedroom clutching the straplessness of the gown, as if her breasts might fly out, shouting, "Surprise!" at any moment. The gown was positively German engineered, however. It fit like a coat of baby oil. But she knew enough of physics to worry that it would slip downward over time, which she told Phoebe.

"Not a chance," Phoebe assured her, and pulled out a roll of double-sided sticky tape. "First, it fits you perfectly. It's constructed to stay up, no matter how you move. And if you're really worried, use this, but I guarantee you won't need it," she added as she tossed the tape to Jane. "Voila: Queen of the Damned."

"As long as I'm not Queen of the Damned hooters," Jane muttered.

"Oh, here is the finishing touch—you simply must have black hair with this costume—this wig will put you totally in character.

You'll need to get some super red lipstick; I've got some in here somewhere along with some stick-on red nails," she chirped, rummaging through her bag. "Here they are, you like?"

"I like. A lot," Mark said. "Jane, you look dangerous in that costume. Phoebe, I really appreciate your bringing the costumes out, especially Jane's. Not too sure about the wig, though."

"Not a problem, Mark. I owe you for the silk thing." To Jane, she advised, "Don't let Mark talk you out of the wig, Jane, it's a costume—not real life." She briskly checked her watch, "I've got to dash back to the city soon. I'm just going to check on your mother before I leave. But, I'll see you both tomorrow night."

Jane returned to the bath to change back into her farm clothes while Phoebe quickly stuffed her bag with various items she'd taken out of it and chatted amiably with Mark. Phoebe had no sooner breezed out of the room, when Jane returned. "Oh no—is Phoebe gone, already?" she asked, "The mesh is stuck on one of the clasps. I can't reach it—I don't want to damage the costume. I can't imagine how it got stuck," she said.

"Yah, she just left. Here, let me see," Mark offered. He gently loosened the mesh from the clasp and pulled it off her shoulders. At the touch of his hands, Jane felt a warm wave move through her. She felt her womb leap into her belly and her face flush. Her eyes lost focus. She turned to face him and breathed in his irresistible woodsy leafy scent, as if he'd spent his days chopping firewood and making fires. She could feel his palpable desire envelope her, as his hands gradually and gently moved from her shoulders down her arms and around her waist. They stood still, as time stood still. She trembled as she met Mark's smoldering gaze. Then he gently wrapped his arms about her, drawing her past the few inches that had separated them, and kissed her deeply, breaking only briefly to shrug off the Dracula cape.

As they lay upon Mark's bed, Jane could not resist her desire and did not wish to. She unbuttoned Mark's shirt as he leaned over her, so full of his own desire and need. She helped him out of his shirt, and they gratefully entered the timeless world of love's passion. They had no thoughts other than to complete each other, to join in the ageless dance, moving as if to music written only for them. In that moment, Jane trusted Mark completely. Whatever her inner turmoil had been or would be, she lost herself in Mark's love. There were no voices in her head, no intrusions from her mother, Sr. Lucille, nor the indictments of past relationships. She trusted Mark, herself, and their bodies' wisdom, so deeply connected to her very soul.

She felt the steadiness of Mark's arms, his gaze penetrating to her innermost being, and heard the tender ache in his calling of her name. She had the unaccountable desire to burst into tears, to laugh, to scream, to gasp, to tell him that she loved him—but she didn't. All of her feelings and desires funneled into the crescendo of a single sigh, "Mark," that trembled out of her. It had been so long since she'd been made love to and had never been brought so satisfactorily and powerfully to conclusion. Afterward, Mark cradled her body in the curve of his own, his arms holding her to him. It was all so impossibly good that Jane wished they could be frozen in this perfect moment.

Until her anxiety began to resurface. "So much for going slow!" she thought. She didn't know whether she loved Mark, or was just infatuated with him. She only knew that she was getting deeper in with him, and that if it didn't work out, it was going to hurt like hell. She needed to get away so that she could think herself strong again. She didn't want to lie in his arms feeling vulnerable, and she had a lesson coming anyway.

As she began to move, Mark instinctively held her more tightly, "Mark," Jane faltered, "I'm so sorry, but I have to get back to the barn. I only blocked two hours for Phoebe."

"Oh, Jane, don't go. Whatever it is, it'll keep. Stay with me."

"I wish I could. But I have a lesson coming, and it's too late to cancel. Believe me, I'd love nothing better than to linger here with you. But, I can't."

She turned toward him, kissed him lightly, and said, "Thank you, Mark. That was wonderful. It truly was. But I have to go."

He protested, but she was out of his bed quickly, throwing her clothes on. She left the costume where it had fallen, almost manic in her need to get away. He jumped out of bed as well, saying, "Jane, don't go. Can't you call Mac? Couldn't he give the lesson?"

"I'm sorry, Mark, it's my job. I couldn't impose on Mac on such short notice. He never gives lessons. But it was lovely being with you. Thanks again."

Chapter Seventeen

Well that was stupid, stupid, stupid! She castigated herself as she walked back to the barn, her knees still knocking. *Thank you? Is that all I could say?* She threw her flannel shirt over her tee to break the wind, and pressed her baseball cap into place. There was no time to change into britches. She fought back tears and rubbed the mists from her eyes. It was a strangely beautiful afternoon, with strong, cool winds sending dark clouds flying past, and frequent instances of sunshine warmly drenching the farm. The air had the scent of oncoming rain, but it was impossible to tell. It might all just blow over.

Jane found herself in a pickle. Never had she connected so fiercely before. Never had she had such a physical explosion. She tripped over a clump of grass on the lawn and almost went sprawling, but managed to right herself at the last moment. Jane had an epiphany: for her, attraction meant desire, and desire sought satisfaction, and satisfaction craved attachment, and attachment unimpeded became love, and love evaporated. For the stronger her love and desire were, the more she feared risking herself, and it was her fear, always, that drove wedges in her relationships. "And that is who you are," she thought to herself, "it isn't fair to Mark, so get hold of yourself, my girl." Why had it been so difficult for her to simply say "no." It was too soon. Was it too soon? Well, it's too late now, she thought.

It was her old fear striking out at her, her father's death, her Catholic guilt, her mother's worry that she'd come home pregnant—or worse, acquire what her mother quaintly called, "a reputation." She could hear her mother now, "who buys the cow when the milk is free." That was the extent of their mother-daughter talks about sex. It was as if they were in some kind of dumbass, sixties girl band, chorusing about loose behavior and a girl's rep, mooning about whether the guy would respect her in the morning. It was all such nonsense. Whatever her inner conflict, it was hers alone, and she needed to ditch it, once and for all. Timing is everything in comedy, she laughed to herself.

She went into the barn and pulled out Ransom's tack. She decided to groom him in his stall. She heard the tractor in the distance with relief, glad that she wouldn't have to face anyone just now. If she hadn't had a lesson coming, she would have stayed with Mark. Should she have called Mac and asked him to take the lesson? Even though Mac never gave lessons, she knew he could easily have stood in for her. He was the far better horseman, for one thing. Of course she should have called Mac. But she'd just panicked. She was too emotional and too afraid to show herself. She despised being thought ridiculous and weak, especially when she was. And she realized that she would sooner push Mark away than allow herself to be vulnerable. Once again, she was shoving her feelings down alone, rather than taking a goddamn risk and talking to Mark.

It would take time for her mind and heart to fade down to something manageable. She led Ransom out to the ring to wait for Mrs. Nelson. She almost tripped again. The grassy field had grown long these past weeks, pushing against the sky and sun to be felt, to be heard. How odd it always seemed that the tender shoots of grass loved the cold weather and the wet. How amazing that the grass survived everything but the heat of the sun. Jane was like the grass, delicate in form, but hearty in her nature, stronger than the oak, resilient. She could easily withstand harsh climates, but wilted in the warmth of the sun as if in a hothouse. But she did not want to wilt in the sun. She wanted to revel in it. She needed the sun's strength and warmth.

She thought about her job and that she had single handedly and without doubt jeopardized the very best situation she'd ever had. And in record time. Not that Mark would fire her; of course, he would never do that. But she might have to quit, if she couldn't get hold of her feelings, especially if things between them didn't work out. The wind picked up, and she could swear she heard Mark whisper her name. She needed to stop her old pattern of forcing men away for fear of being hurt, or she would have to accept the cold and damp of a heart that shriveled in the sun.

She gave Mrs. Nelson her lesson in a daze. "Up, down" Jane heard herself repeating in a monotone as Mrs. Nelson attempted to master the concept of posting to trot, at a walk. "Up, down" she found herself rhythmically repeating, as visions of herself and Mark danced teasingly before her. She was greatly relieved when the lesson ended. She cleaned and put up the tack and gave Ransom an extra special rub down. She walked slowly back to her house, knowing how grateful her body would be for a bath and a good night's sleep.

All will be well, she told herself. After all of her emotional upheaval, she chose acceptance—everything was already what it was and would be what it would be. And that would be fine. And either way, she would have her place the sun.

Chapter Eighteen

Mark was utterly baffled by Jane's having left so unceremoniously. He didn't know what to make of it. He knew she was shy, but he thought they'd broken through that. He had felt full and content with her. And when she left, she took the fullness away, leaving Mark disheartened with an empty feeling in his chest. He thought that perhaps she still worried about his being, technically, her boss. He wished that he hadn't let his desire override his recent decision, and her request, to take things slow. He wished that he had told her what he was feeling. But he didn't want to scare her off. They hadn't known each other very long, after all—only a couple of months. He didn't want to spring a ridiculously premature marriage proposal on her. He wasn't sure he'd even won her yet, "For Chrissake, Mark, you're going to drive her off if you keep coming on so strong," he chided himself.

He'd give her some time to gather her thoughts, and then he'd somehow make this right. Mark had never experienced complications with women, he pursued them, and they generally enjoyed his company, and things never got serious. He never wanted them to. It was different with Jane. He had wanted her, and he had had her. But the expected relief he usually experienced after sleeping with a woman was not forthcoming. In fact, his desire had intensified. He wanted her more now, somehow, and found himself worrying about what she was thinking and how she was feeling.

It occurred to him that he'd never taken a woman to his place, not even in the city. He always stayed at the woman's place. And he was the one who always itched to leave. He often made himself stay the night with women out of politeness, but there were times when, God forgive him, he jumped out of bed with some lame ass excuse to the woman whose body had lately served his purpose. Well, now he'd gotten a taste of his own medicine, not, he thought, that Jane intended it that way. Still, she sped out so fast, she ditched her own shadow.

As he watched her make her way to the barn, he breathed her name. He had all but mentally traded the Porsche for something with four doors—oh god, a minivan. What more was there left for him to experience? Alone, he'd flown planes, sky dived, raced cars, hiked mountains. He'd had more women than he cared to count. He thought of Phillips and his wife and children. Phillips, who had done none of these things to Mark's knowledge, but was contented.

After a shower and some food, he went for a walk. The afternoons had begun to darken earlier, and he saw Jane in the outdoor arena with her lesson. The clouds rolled over, and the sun dashed in and out behind them. Would Jane accept him for the long haul? He laughed at himself, suddenly feeling like a woman in a comedy, only he was the one saying, "tick tock, Jane, t-i-c-k, t-o-c-k." If he was ever going to have a family, he thought, there was no time to lose. He'd already let too many years go by.

The tall grass and the taller alfalfa of the fields in the distance moved in slow sheets from the pressure of the wind, and the shadows of the clouds over the waving fields put Mark in mind of Van Gogh, so much passion—"it's no wonder he cut off his ear, poor bastard," Mark thought, just as a swiftly swirling rook of starlings sped through the skies like schools of fish in the ocean. Their rapid adjustments crossing the sky back and forth mimicked the waving of the alfalfa, and Mark felt his world altering and shifting. He saw the bright promise of loving Jane, of sharing his life with her, making children with her, gumming their oatmeal together in old age.

He went home and poured a short whiskey and coiffed it. It was pointless to ruminate any further. He needed to talk to Jane.

As he traversed the distance to her house in long strides, he called her on the cell and asked if she'd see him. She was waiting at the door for him as he closed the distance between them.

She had just emerged from the bath and was still in her robe.

"May I come in, Jane?" Mark smiled.

"Please do," she politely replied.

"Can I get you something to eat or drink?" she asked.

"Actually, I was wondering if we could just talk," and hearing Rachel and Abby animatedly conversing in the kitchen, added, "privately. We could go out, if you like," he offered.

"Ben and Abby and Rachel have plans for a movie. He's on his way over. I'm a little tired, actually. I was getting ready for bed," and seeing his mien lower, added, "but, we can talk in my room, if you like. I'd like that."

They sat cross-legged upon Jane's bed, and Mark took her hands in his. "I missed you after you left this afternoon, Jane," he began.

"Oh, yes," she said, coloring, "I'm so sorry about that. But I'm glad you're here now. I wanted to talk to you, too."

"Do you want to go first?" he asked.

Jane, steeling herself for whatever Mark wanted to say, invited him to speak first.

"I don't know exactly how to begin—I feel as if my mind has been swirling since I met you. First of all," he vowed, "you're beautiful, Jane. I could look at you forever." Encouraged by her blush and smile, Mark continued, "and I love how quirky you are," he laughed. "You're so...unpredictable. And you don't pretend to be anything you're not. I love your honesty and your kindness. And you're smart, and..."

Mark paused, and smiled broadly, "Jane, I'm in love with you. I know you don't want to go too fast, and every time we're together, I know I have, we have. I want there to be more to us than just great sex." Mark looked down at Jane's hands in his. "Jane, I'm forty. I don't want to scare you off, but I've never felt about anyone the way I've been feeling about you." Mark looked up into Jane's open face and pointed out, "We're not kids. I know what I want for the first time in a long time." Mark saw Jane's brow knitting into a frown and, fearing that he'd said too much added, "Just tell me that I've got a chance, Jane. If we're not on the same page…"

"Mark," Jane said as tears began to form, "we are so most definitely on the same page," she said, taking his face in her hands and kissing him. "I was afraid I was the only one feeling this way. I'm so sorry, I should have trusted more."

"Jane," he said tenderly, pulling her onto his lap, "please don't ever be afraid of me or of us. I love you, and I will love you tomorrow and the next day, and the day after that. I've never been a religious man, Jane, but the way I feel, it's like praying, and hoping, and knowing all at the same time."

And then he loved her. He loved her with his body. He loved her with his heart. He loved her with his soul. He loved her unreservedly, and all of their confusion lifted in the wisdom of their bodies.

Chapter Nineteen

Jane woke up alone, the fire Mark had made was burning brightly and cheerfully. And then she smelled coffee and bacon. She hadn't heard Abby or Rachel stir—it was still early for either of them to rise. She hoped that she and Mark had not disturbed them during the night. She threw on her robe and rubbed the solid oak door—*hmm, pretty thick. I think we're good here.* As she went downstairs, she followed the scent of coffee, a spiritual experience at that hour, and bacon and eggs.

"I thought you might be hungry," Mark said smiling at her. "I'm starved. Do you like your eggs over easy?"

"Anyway is fine," Jane yawned. "So, did you sleep well?" she asked with a shy smile.

"When I slept, yah," he laughed, as he put a plate of bacon and toast in front of her.

"And you cook, too. This is great," she said, taking a slice of perfectly crisp bacon. "Thank you."

"You're not going to thank me for sex again, are you?" Mark said, sliding an egg on her toast.

"Are you kidding me?" she laughed. "I'm having an award made, like an Oscar, only more phallic—if that's even possible."

"Why, Jane O'Hara, I'm seeing a new side of you. I'm impressed."

As Mark poured more coffee, Jane asked, "So, what are you going to do today? Anything important?"

"Well, I'll need to be on deck this afternoon for the party, but I was hoping we could spend most of the day together. What's your schedule like?"

"Not too bad, actually. Just morning chores. No lessons scheduled, in honor of the party. Why," she smiled, "what did you have in mind?"

"Nothing much," he said.

And when she'd had taken precisely five bites of her breakfast, he took her by the hand, and they raced up the stairs back to her bedroom.

*

Jane spent the entire day with Mark, and in between barn chores they ate, and talked, and made love. When they weren't occupied with each other physically, they enjoyed forging the emotional connection they'd begun so brilliantly the night before. As they lay in Jane's bed, Mark held her, his arms circled around her protectively. "Jane," he said, "you never did get a chance to tell me what was on your mind, last night. I feel guilty. You said you wanted to talk, too, but I kind of took over."

"Oh," she dismissed, "it was nothing—just my crazy fear, Mark. You brushed the clouds away."

"I'm glad of that, but what were you afraid of?"

"Nothing…really," she winced, recalling her thoughts yesterday.

"Something, I think. You can tell me."

She looked up at him, contented that she could tell him anything. "Well," she began, "I didn't think you could ever really love me, and I was so freaking head over heels for you. I let the old voices in my head rule me. I didn't trust you or myself. And, I was afraid that the sex was so good that it would block out anything else from developing. I should have had more faith in you, Mark. I'm sorry I didn't."

"Is that all?" he said, and squeezed her reassuringly. "Not long ago, you might have been right, Jane. But that's all in the past, love. I promise you that."

"Oh, speaking of the past," Jane blurted out, "do we need to speak of it? The idea of reviewing past relationships makes me want to ralph."

"Oh, God no," Mark pronounced emphatically. "Let's just say we come with experiences from which we learned all good lessons. Does that work for you?"

"Perfectly," Jane murmured with relief.

As the afternoon waned, and the time drew near for them to part briefly until the party, they sealed their belief in each other, in love, and in their bright hope for the future. "God, Jane," Mark breathed, "I can't get enough of you."

Chapter Twenty

Abby called out eagerly, "Jane, hurry up, let's see it!" Abby, who had never celebrated Halloween as a child, took to the holiday like a duck to water. Jane emerged awkwardly in full regalia, including the wig, lipstick, and the blood-red nails that Phoebe had provided. "Whatdya think?" she asked nervously.

"I think that outfit is illegal in forty-eight states. Girl, you look absolutely smashing in that costume. Has Mark seen it?"

"Oh yes," Jane said, recollecting what it had led to. As she considered her reflection in the mirror, she said, "It kind of begs for a pole, though, don't you think?"

"You might get lucky later," Abby joked. "So, sweetie, I've been meaning to ask you, but is it okay if I start seeing Ben?"

"Of course!" Jane said, happily shocked. "When did this all happen?"

"Well, nothing has 'happened' yet, but at the movie—he held my hand," she said, placing said hand dramatically to her heart, and biting her lower lip, she laughed, "I may never wash it again. Seriously, he's pretty wonderful. Tell me I look like a sick kitty, who needs to call a vet."

Just then Rachel entered and teased, "Hey, good pole dancing outfit."

"Rachel," Jane said, laughing, "I swear, sometimes you turn on that clairvoyance like a faucet on purpose."

"Nah, I heard you talking."

Jane looked at Abby and declared, "We gotta get her a boyfriend."

Just then, the doorbell rang. "I'll get it—it might be Ben!" Abby said, dashing down the stairs.

Rachel impulsively kissed Jane and observed, "Don't look now, but you're glowing."

"What about you, Rachel, are you sad that your best buds are hooking up?"

"No, not at all. I'm thrilled for both of you."

"What about Ben and Abby—is there a good shot there?"

Rachel closed her eyes a moment and smiled, "I see much dancing at the wedding—a wild Jewish affair, you understand!" she added, laughing.

But Jane sensed something not quite right in Rachel's countenance. Still, she didn't want to probe lest it concern her. She didn't want her spirits dampened with any vague misgivings and quickly changing the subject, asked, "So, what do you think? Gorgeous or gruesome?" extending her arms and spinning around.

"C'mon," Rachel replied, "Quit yer fishing. You're totally gorgeous, and you know it."

Chapter Twenty-one

Veronica didn't think much of Halloween dress up. She supposed it was because she was so often photographed in outlandish costumes and makeup. And she especially reviled this particular Halloween for obvious reasons: she was readying herself to crash a party where she had not been invited, and was intending to confront its host. She peered into her mirror and brushed her hair, so black it shone blue in the light. She lightly powdered her porcelain skin, leaving off any blush. Pale suited her. She applied her signature crimson lipstick.

On the bed lay her Deringer, in dark contrast against the white bedspread. Her black, jeweled evening bag appeared curiously mated to the black gun next to it. She placed the Deringer inside the purse and put the strap of the purse on her shoulder as the doorman rang to announce that her limo had arrived. She slid into its blackness in silence. The driver had the address and held the door for her. Passing through Elizabeth, the sulfurous smell of rotting petrol-chemicals got into the car and attached itself to the linings of her nasal passages. She could not get rid of the smell the rest of the way into New Jersey. Even when the car was well away and in the country, the stench rode with her and clung to her.

She was not well. She felt nauseous and depressed. She stared out the window of the car at the passing lights and the lines of the turnpike, each of which was accompanied by a monotonous bumping of the undercarriage. She was so tired. Veronica, super model, abandoned child, beautiful, ugly duckling, who could have any man, rejected, pregnant. She closed her eyes and pulled her coat about her. She felt her evening bag and the small lady's weapon it concealed. It occurred to her that she could stop. She could knock on the glass barrier that separated her from the driver and simply ask him to turn the car around. Maybe he was a nice guy, and she could take him out to dinner somewhere. And then, they could go back to New York. Maybe a guy like that would fall in love with her and appreciate her. She wondered if he was married. *Probably. Probably had ten kids, too.*

She knocked on the glass. "Excuse me," she said, "do you know how much longer it will take?"

"Not long, now, Miss. Maybe ten, fifteen minutes."

There was something in the way he called her "Miss" that was so impersonal, so cold, it enraged her. She knew that she could not turn back. She stared at the back of his head. He was probably about Mark's age, late thirties or early forties. His neck swelled slightly above his collar. Beefy. His hands on the steering wheel were beefy too. His fingers like disgusting sausages wound around the wheel.

He would not have dinner with her. He would dump her at Mark's and later, he would return to his wife and ten kids. When he got home, he'd mention his pathetic last passenger, "Guess who I rode out to the country, tonight, hon." And his wife would say, indifferently, "Who?" And he'd reply, "That famous super model—you know, Veronica. Man, she was messed up looking."

She inhaled suddenly and deeply. She resolved to have her vengeance against the driver's imagined pity, and his imagined wife's imagined disdain. She would stand up to Mark and make him pay for hurting her. And all the men of the world who had already left or would leave her, if they had the chance, would know that she was not to be trifled with. All those thoughtless men with no feelings, no conscience in them, they were everywhere. Talking about how beautiful she was and how crazy.

Yes, her plan was a good one. She continued to ride in silence to Lamington Road. She was committed. There was no turning back, now.

Chapter Twenty-two

Mark was on duty early at the house. Manuel, Mac, Phillips, and several men from the job crews assembled early as well. They all had cell phones to talk to each other or to call the police in case anything went wrong.

"Phillips, you watch the door and the east portion of the living room. Manuel, you take your men and circulate among the guests and keep an eye on the open bar, especially for those returning too frequently. And Mac, you watch the gypsy corner in the library," he instructed.

The men nodded to their assignments, and as they were on holiday pay, eagerly accepted their duty. Except for Phillips, the men all wore black shirts and pants, to blend in with the servers and bartenders. Mark lent Mac one of his black jackets, as they were similar in frame. Mark implored Mac, always so serious and responsible, to try to enjoy himself at the party and to try not to look quite so much like a secret serviceman.

At four p.m., the first of the early visitors to the farm, young couples with small children, began to shyly appear. The pumpkins, jack o'lanterns, witches, and Halloween lights about the house were all lit. Eerie music and smoking cauldrons, skeletons, monsters, and all of the wonderful Halloween ornaments were in full effect. Phillips and his wife and children were all dressed as pirates with eye patches, bandanas, baggy pants, muslin shirts, and fake scabbards at their sides.

At one point, there seemed to be hundreds of children present. The bandleader had them formally march about, ostensibly to choose a winner. One child was dressed as a jelly bean jar—a clear plastic bag holding different colored balloons surrounded him. There were the assorted animal costumes, princesses, tramps, angels, and a variety of little witches. The best of these was a pert young girl dressed in a trim black miniature business suit, wearing a pointed hat, a black bird stitched to the shoulder of her jacket, carrying a small black briefcase labeled, "boardroom witch." It was impossible to choose a winner. Mark presented each of the parents with a bond for their children, and for immediate gratification, there was an endless supply of candy. And for the parents, an assortment of refreshments to reinforce them through the rigors of their Halloween celebrations.

As the young families began to disperse to continue their trick-or-treating elsewhere, the more serious party-going townspeople began to arrive. This population of celebrants was decidedly more adult and enthusiastic at their hob-nobbing and alcohol reinforcement. Jane, Abby, Ben, and Rachel joined the party as this group of party-goers reached its maximum, and just before the limousines from afar began to arrive.

As soon as he saw Jane, Mark came over to her. He wore his black cape and had rather generously splattered food dye on his white shirt—not the decorous collar markings Phoebe had suggested. "Subtle, Mark. I'm feeling much more *Texas Chainsaw Massacre* now," Jane said.

"Well, I was going more for Blade than Buffy. Who wants a bloodless vampire?" he teased. He smiled and nodded to the group, and whirled Jane around in his arms. "I missed you. How long has it been?"

"Infinity!" Jane laughed.

"I vant to suck your blood," he joked.

"And I vant to suck your… award," she snickered, coloring at her own crassness.

"Why, Jane, I'm shocked, you vixen! I knew I loved you," Mark chortled.

The band switched to a slow dance, and Mark didn't miss a beat. He swept Jane onto the dance floor.

The party was in full swing. The wine flowed liberally, Jane's black martinis were a huge success, the food was ample and impeccable, and the two bands, extraordinary. Then the limousines began to arrive and the many clients, professional acquaintances, staff, and friends from New York brightened the party further with their glamorous presence. Their costumes seemed more extravagant, their relationships more purposeful, somehow.

When the swing bandleader announced that it was time for the bachelor and bachelorette drawing, five men and sixteen women had put their names in the hat. But the last couple called were Mark Hannon and Jane O'Hara. Mark squeezed Jane's hand—"I cheated," he cheerfully confessed. "I hope you don't mind." And, of course, she didn't.

As the music began and couples once again hit the dance floor, Jane and Mark decided to pop into the gypsy corner to see if Rachel needed anything. They had not seen her all evening. They chatted briefly with Mac at the library door. "How's it going?" Jane asked.

Mac stood impassively against the wall. "No screams. I guess she's all right. She's been busy though."

"Take a break, Mac," Mark offered. "Go get a plate of food before the New York crowd scarfs it all up. We'll keep an eye on things in the gypsy corner for you." Mac didn't need extra encouragement and disappeared in search of refreshments, as Jane and Mark breezed into the library, holding hands. They plunked down on the couch in front of Rachel who sat at the table with a crystal ball set on it.

"So, how's it going in here? Mac says a ton of people have been coming in and out," Jane said.

"I'm exhausted," Rachel groaned, pulling off her wart and blackened tooth. "I've never given so many readings—my pad is full. I hate to say it, Mark, but I'm going to have to close down the gypsy corner soon. My psychic membranes are swollen," she moaned, rubbing her temples.

"Blech. Sounds nasty—shall I make you some tea?" Jane offered.

"Oh hell no! Get me one of those martinis," she dictated, "and hold the espresso. I need mother's milk."

Mark went to get Rachel a martini, while Jane encouraged her to close up shop for the night. "C'mon," Jane said. "You're done here."

"No, not yet. There's one other reading. I've been waiting for her."

"Waiting for who, honey?"

"Mark's ex-girlfriend," she said darkly. "She's close by. I can sense her." They both looked through the door at the crowds of people dancing, laughing loudly, conversing, eating and drinking in the living room adjacent to the library.

"There must be two hundred people in there," Jane calculated. "Well, sweetie, you think she'll swing by for a reading?"

"I know she will. Remember when I read Mark? This is the room I saw her in."

Just then Mark returned with the martini and placed it in front of Rachel. "Here you go Madame Babushka. Drink up," he ordered, cheerfully.

"Mmmm," she happily crooned, sipping her martini, "forget about Jane, marry me!"

"What's your view of bigamy, Jane?" he teased, and seeing her mock rueful look, added, "Okay, okay, I'm all mahogany, I mean monogamy," he laughed and put his arm around Jane. He drew little circles on her shoulder and pouted handsomely until she laughed.

"Mark," Rachel said, "I took the liberty of going into that old run-down mansion again the other day. I hope you don't mind."

"Not at all, Jane told me you were interested in renting it. It's yours, if you want it. No charge. But it's kind of a mess, isn't it?"

"Well it needs airing," she said. "Psychically speaking, it's rotten fish."

"Manuel will work on it, but only during the day. He's more superstitious than I thought. I always thought the whole story was just a myth the locals invented to keep their kids out of the place."

"Right," added Jane. "You know, Timmy scraped his knee, ergo the place is haunted...right?" she looked at Rachel hopefully.

"'Fraid not, guys. The place is totally haunted. And," she paused, sipping her martini, "it could use a coat of paint. But it's a great place, if I can get the bad out of it. It's what our grandmothers would have called 'swell' or 'swank' at our age. I'd love to restore it. What about Mac? He doesn't seem to be afraid of anything. Would he help, do you think?"

"If Jane can give him time away from the barn. What do you think, Jane?"

"It's up to Mac. I don't mind sharing."

"Maggie, our Realtor, won't even show the place. She says it creeps her out to set foot in it."

"She'll be the first test case, then, when I've cured it—the canary in the *mind*, as it were," Rachel said.

"So, what's your plan?" asked Jane.

"I'm not sure yet. But, it'll come to me. I hate the idea of a séance—even I find séances spooky. I'll keep you posted."

"Well, if you need us, we'll help," Mark offered.

"Are you crazy?" Jane broke in. "Séance? That's a hole-done-choke multiverse of 'no' for me. Horse whisperer here, not ghost whisperer," Jane said, emphatically.

"I'll talk her into it, Rachel, don't worry," Mark winked.

Abby and Ben whisked in with more drinks and a plate of food for Rachel. "I thought you might be hungry," Abby said to Rachel. Then tossing back her third black martini, she complimented Jane on her "little espresso thingies," momentarily unable to recollect the word "martini," and luxuriously stretched out, looking less like cat woman and more like an actual cat flopped on a chair.

"Thank God you're here. Save me," Jane said to Ben and Abby.

"You bet, honey," Abby said fuzzily, "what are we saving you from?"

"Ghosts!" Jane winced. "And a séance."

Oh, cool!" Abby hiccoughed.

Ben glanced from Abby to Jane, in obvious commiseration with Jane and mumbled something about *The Exorcist* and not asking for trouble.

"I just want to assist whatever spirits are wrecking the old mansion to leave so I can live in it. You know, help them move on into the light and all," Rachel insisted.

"Couldn't we just call Jennifer Love Hewitt?" Jane asked.

As they discussed whether to séance or not to séance, an angry, larger-than-life, Veronica-shaped silhouette, her hand shoved in her purse, and her purse held out at arm's length in front of her violently filled the doorway, like *The Thing from Another World*.

Chapter Twenty-three

Mark was in a panic. He couldn't believe his eyes: Veronica held the strap of her purse with one hand, the other plunged into it. She withdrew her hand for a second, to reveal the gun, and quickly plunged it back again, as she glanced over her shoulder and kicked the door shut behind her.

Abby was so drunk, she was the only one not to see the gun, nor to understand the importance of Veronica's showing up. "Who's that?" she asked Rachel in a loud whisper.

"Shhhh. Shut up, Abby," Rachel hissed.

"Veronica," Mark stepped toward her, "what do you want?"

"Veronica!" Abby pronounced, "uh-oh."

"Stay right where you are, Mark" Veronica said. As she locked the door, she demanded, "Who are these people?"

Trying to protect his friends, especially Jane, Mark lied, "I don't know them. I just came in to get away from the party, and they were here. Let them go, we can talk."

Ignoring Mark, Veronica commanded, "Everyone, cell phones in the fireplace, now!"

Jane, ignoring Mark's pressure on her arm urging her to remain seated, began to rise, diverting Veronica's gaze in her direction. "Who are you, and why are you made up to look like me?" Mark groaned inwardly. *Why, oh why couldn't she have gone as Darla, the cute blonde cheerleading vampire? I knew that wig was a mistake.*

"She's my sister," Rachel piped up.

Briefly examining Jane, Veronica sneered, "I don't like you. You look like a cheap, slut version of me. Sit down and shut up if you want to live," she threatened, shaking her purse at Jane, which caused Abby to drunkenly giggle. Everyone flung Abby a look as Veronica placed a chair in front of the locked door.

"Veronica, let them go. They don't have anything to do with us."

"'Us,' Mark? So there's an 'us' now? It was hard to tell, what with the not answering my calls a hundred times."

"I don't feel so good," Abby said, looking paler by the second. "I think I'm gonna hurl."

Ignoring Abby, Mark prevaricated, "I was going to call you, Veronica, I swear. I was just waiting for the right moment," he said lamely.

"Like when the big hand hit 'Freezes Over' on the clock in Hell?" she spat back.

"Oh my God, oh my God," Abby moaned. Ben rubbed the back of her neck to soothe her.

"Fuck you Mark, you lying sack of shit!" Veronica shouted.

And with that, Abby made good on her promise and lurching forward proceeded to vomit copiously on the library rug, as poor Ben held her hair for her.

In an odd moment of unanimous consensus, everyone grimaced with disgust.

Trying to focus her vision on the Veronica in the middle, Abby slurred, "Dya mind if I lie down somewhere? I'm gonna boot again if I don't."

"Gross!" Veronica bleated, and pointing to the window seat said, "Over there, where I can keep an eye on you."

"I've seen you in *Vogue*—you're Armani's favorite model, right?" Rachel said quietly. Mark mentally applauded her calm approach to distracting Veronica.

"What is your point? Are we friends?" she asked sarcastically.

"You're much more beautiful in person, that's all." Rachel said, hoping to mollify Veronica and diffuse her anger.

Veronica hesitated, "Thank you. Nice of you to say that, especially under the circumstances." Then she turned to Mark and asked acridly, "What about you, Mark? Do you find me more beautiful in person?" As she spoke, she lowered the purse, and took out the pistol, waving it in front of her. Not waiting for Mark to answer, her attention was once again drawn to Jane.

"You," she spat at Jane, "yah, you. What's the deal with the costume? Are you trying to look like me?"

"No," Jane stuttered, "I'm supposed to be the Queen of the Damned."

"Exactly my point," Veronica muttered.

As Veronica looked more intently at Jane, she recognized her dress, "That's Phoebe Rich's Donatella Versace design. I remember it distinctly," she sneered at Mark. "So, you don't know these people, huh?"

Mark started to rise, but Veronica quickly pointed the gun at Jane and commanded, "Sit your ass down, or I'll pump your girlfriend," she yelled.

Mark quickly resumed his seat. "What do you want of me, Veronica?"

"Much" she imitated Marley's ghost in *The Christmas Carol* and seeing Mark's blank expression, sneered, "Shit. Read much, Ebenezer?"

"Please just let them go," Mark pleaded.

"Wrong thing to say, Mark. Whatever you want to protect, I want to hurt. My guess is that Suzy Veronica Wannabe here is your new girl. Why else would Phoebe put her in Versace? You're such an idiot, Mark. I'm a model, asshole, if there's one thing I know it's fashion."

Veronica slumped visibly, as if tired of her own charade. "You could have had me, Mark, the real Veronica. Why go to the trouble of dressing up some dumbass waitress?" she hissed.

Jane slid her wig off and put it on the gypsy table before saying, "I work here—I'm the barn manager. Mark was just being kind to me. The costume was Phoebe's idea, that's all."

"For real?" Veronica retorted. "You're the *barn* manager? Do you milk his cows or something?"

"Horse barn," Jane said. "I take care of the horses. These are my friends. We came in here to take a breather from the party, and Mark just came in, too. There's nothing more to it."

"Oh, in that case, I'm really sorry," Veronica said sarcastically, "but you still can't go. I can't have you calling the cops. Not yet." Veronica glared at Mark, her voice rising, "Mark, I came here to kick every square inch of your extremely deserving ass. Phoebe told me you were a player and that you dumped every woman you ever dated, but I figured, 'that won't happen to me. I'm *Veronica*, for Chrissake.' But I was wrong."

"Veronica, I'm—" Mark broke in.

"Shut the fuck up!" she shouted. "I'm not finished yet. You think you can just use me, get me *pregnant*—yes, that's right, asshole, I'm pregnant—and walk away? Stand up, motherfucker!"

Mark stood up to take the bullet he believed she intended to deliver, when he saw Jane also jump up like lightening, hurling herself toward Veronica. Mark was able to grab her arm and swing her behind him, as she shouted, "Don't shoot!"

"Hell yah! Mark," Veronica said, impressed, "your staff is loyal. I'll give you that."

At that moment, Rachel snatched Jane's wig from the table and threw it at Veronica, and Ben started to rush her. The wig was too lightweight to travel far and instead wafted for a short distance and fell short of its target. It did create some mischief, however, sailing just speedily enough to get tangled in Ben's feet, tripping him, as he stormed toward Veronica.

At the same time, Mark was relieved to see Mac burst through the locked door like a wrecking ball. And when Veronica looked back, he rushed her. A chaos of arms and legs all intent on overcoming Veronica ensued. Everyone ran at her, and as Rachel screamed, "Look out!" the gun gave out a muffled explosion and flew out of Veronica's hand as she was tackled. On the way down, she hit her head on the side table.

Chapter Twenty-four

Outside the library, the swing band and the rock band were showing off their skills, and the energy of the party was at its peak. Almost no one, therefore, had heard the gun go off. And those few who had heard something did not recognize the noise as a shot. Two people had noticed Mac force the library door in, but they had assumed it was merely stuck and attached no interpretations of danger to it. The music played loudly, the wine flowed amply, and everyone in good humor noticed nothing awry.

A few euphoric partiers nearby peered into the library with mild curiosity at the apparent scuffle, but Mark went to the door quickly and shooed them back. "Everything okay?" a woman slurred as a few others loitered about with inquiringly raised eyebrows.

"Nothing to worry about," Mark dissembled. "Madame Babushka threw a cherry bomb into the fireplace for fun. Just a Halloween prank. Bangin' party, eh?" he added, as if crazy slang would derail further inquiry. Changing the subject, he added for lack of anything better to say, "Enjoy the party, folks." *Move along, now, nothing to see here.* He picked up the pieces of the antique Windsor chair Mac splintered when he'd forced the door open.

Ben muttered apologetically to Mark, "Sorry, man. I didn't mean to trip."

Mark nodded and gave Ben an understanding look. "Next time there's a gun pointed at us, I'm sure you'll do better."

Abby yawned broadly and then settled back down.

Mac looked at Mark earnestly, "She hit her head pretty good. We should call an ambulance."

"We should call a cop," Ben exclaimed, still frightened. "She held us at gunpoint!" Ben was neither a violent nor a vengeful man, but it was clear to Mark that his nerves were understandably rattled. An innate caretaker, he nonetheless picked up one of the martinis and sprinkled Veronica's face with it and lightly rapped her cheeks to bring her around.

Mac ordered, "We're takin' her to the hospital, now. Mark, can you help me get her up?"

As they lifted her gently, Rachel picked up the gun, "This thing's an antique, for God's sake. The chambers are empty. I don't think it was loaded. It's hardly more than a cap gun."

Veronica muttered, "I didn't want to kill him. I wanted him to be afraid. Like I am. He should have just returned my calls. I'm pregnant with his kid," she sobbed.

Mac looked sternly at Mark. "She's got a point against you, there."

They decided that they would all take Veronica to the hospital out the back door of the library and through the back hallway. "Veronica, can you walk?" Mark asked.

"My heart's broken, not my legs," she said bitterly.

They grabbed the nearest limo, telling the driver it was an emergency, and Mark gave directions for Somerset Medical Center.

Mark and Mac walked Veronica into the hospital while the others stayed in the car. Once admitted, Mac volunteered to stay, "You go back with the others and take care of the party, boss. I'll call when we're ready to leave." Mark trudged back to the car. *Would this night ever end?*

When they were close to the farm, Jane asked wearily, "Would you mind just dropping me at the farmhouse, Mark? It's late. The party's over."

"Abby's done in too, Mark," Ben observed. "Jane, I'll help you and Rachel put her to bed."

Mark wanted so badly to speak with Jane. He needed her to somehow help him through Veronica's bombshell. Without Jane, he was lost. But he couldn't think of any argument other than his own selfish need to persuade her to stay with him. He didn't deserve her kindness or her forgiveness. Suddenly, the integrity he'd prattled about all his life seemed worthless. He'd been reckless. Irresponsible. He'd made a child with a woman whose last name he couldn't remember, for God's sake, for which he would pay dearly and not only in financial terms—that meant nothing to him. He'd created this child, and he would step up to the plate, no matter what that meant. How ironic all of his previous shilly-shallying about his freedom and his integrity seemed now. If Jane left him, well, she'd be well rid of him. It was for the best. *I won't drag her into this mess I've made. It's my responsibility.*

Chapter Twenty-five

The party crowd had substantially thinned. He caught Phillips' eye, and gestured for him to come to the library. Mark respected Phillips more than anyone he knew. When push came to shove, he valued Phillips' counsel even more than that of his parents.

Mark registered the look on Phillips' face as he entered the library, as he looked from the broken Windsor chair to Mark. Mark had no idea what to say or where to start. He had just come to the conclusion that he wanted a family with Jane, and now he was to be the father of Veronica's child. Exhaling, he said more to himself than Phillips, "Have I always been a fool?" Then, looking directly at Phillips, he said, "I just found out from my ex-girlfriend that I'm going to be a father. With Jane, it would have all made sense. But Veronica…how am I going to be a father, Phillips, to a child whose mother I didn't care for and barely knew? And, Jane…this will change everything for her, I have no doubt. How will I do this without her?"

"You'll find a way, Mark, and Jane will find her way, too," he said. But to Mark the words sounded like an accusation, and he felt a new pang of guilt and sorrow.

"Can I ask you a personal question, Phillips?" and when he nodded, "Are you happy?"

"Yes." Phillips said. "My wife is my soul mate. I love my children. They fill my life with laughter and surprise."

"Did you always want to be a family man, Phillips?"

"Of course not!" he acknowledged. "At twenty, I wanted to be a pilot. You knew I was in the Air Force before coming here, right? But my vision wasn't sharp enough—astigmatism. So I had to give up that dream."

"Do you regret the life you might have had?"

"Never. We only regret the absence of something when we feel empty. I feel full. Look at me, Mark. I'm dressed up like a pirate. I couldn't have done that in the Air Force."

"In a year or two," Mark surmised, "I'll be dancing about the place in a Santa Claus suit."

"Yah, now there's a visual," Phillips laughed in sympathy adding, "You're going to be a father. You didn't seek it, didn't plan for it. But there you have it, anyway. My advice? Throw yourself into your child's life. Give every ounce of what's inside of you. Commit, and have no regrets."

"Even if it means looking ridiculous in a pirate costume?"

"Welcome to the Daddy Club," Phillips commiserated.

"Thank you, Phillips." Mark nodded admiringly. "I want to be like you when I grow up. Would you do me a kindness and ask my parents to come in to me? I can't face anyone else just now."

*

Mark wanted to tell his parents about Veronica's pregnancy—carefully editing out her anger management issues. He'd hoped the news that Robert and Nora were to be grandparents would make them happy. But, as he thought it through, he couldn't even tell them when to expect the happy event. Then he thought of all their questions—who was the mother, how had he met her, did he love her or intend to marry her, and a dozen other questions. And then there was Jane. How would he explain to them where Jane fit in, when he didn't know himself any longer?

He was weary to the bone before he began. His parents, too, looked tired. Surely it would be a kindness to tell them tomorrow, to prepare to be happy for their sakes if not for his own. It was selfish to tell them tonight, to seek their comfort for his fears. He sacrificed his desire to once more be their son, their child, to let them solve this problem for him, as if he'd skinned his knee or failed an algebra test. For one last time, he yearned to be their son and not someone else's father. But he did not give into it.

As they waited for him to speak, Nora nervously glanced at Robert and finally broke the silence. "Mark, what is it, dear? You're scaring me. Are you in some kind of trouble?"

"No, I'm not in any trouble. I just wanted you to know how much I love you. I don't think I've ever told you or not often enough, anyway."

Nora, visibly relieved, leaned over and hugged Mark as she hadn't done since he was twelve. "That's sweet of you to say, isn't it Robert?" Robert, far less sentimental than Nora, nodded.

Chapter Twenty-six

Mark rose with the first light of dawn. He needed to see Jane. He gathered the girls' bags, and jackets. He waited for as long as he could, but at seven a.m., he went to the farmhouse. He knocked lightly, and Rachel answered in her nightgown and bare feet.

"Jane's gone, Mark." Rachel said. "She must have left shortly after we all went to bed. I woke up before dawn and felt something strange, so I came down to the kitchen. She left a note saying that she needed to get away to think. She asked me to make sure the horses were taken care of. She said that if Mac were still at the hospital with Veronica, you'd know what to do. She didn't say where she was going."

"Do you know where she went, Rachel? Can you feel anything?" Mark pleaded.

"I don't know where her mother lives, Mark, but I'm guessing that's where she went."

"I'll find her. What's her mother's name?"

"Mom," Rachel prevaricated, and then relented, "I think it's Emily. But Mark, don't track her. She needs to work things out for herself. I feel that much strongly. You need to honor her decision and trust her. I know that's hard." And handing him a second note, "This is for you," she said and watched Mark silently as he read:

Dear Mark,

I'm sorry to take the coward's way and leave like this. But I need to think about what Veronica's news means. You're going to be a father. You will need to make a lot of decisions. Things have moved at light speed for us, Mark, and I need to slow down.

Please don't try to find me. I'll call when I've sorted things out.
Love,
Jane.

Mark's expression fell. He shoved the note in his pocket. Rachel looked with the utmost compassion at him. "I wish I knew what to say, Mark. Do you want to talk? Would you like some coffee?" Mark thanked her, but bolted out of the farmhouse, a place so recently filled with happy memories. He was visibly shaken.

*

"I'm sorry," the doctor said to a disappointed and tearful Veronica as she lay in the narrow hospital bed, "but you are not pregnant. Home pregnancy tests are ninety-seven percent reliable, but there are occasional false positives."

She rubbed her arms and shivered, "Well, now everyone will know all about 'crazy Veronica' who thought she was pregnant and brandished a goddamn art object at her scornful lover," she looked sorrowfully at the young intern, "Strangely, I don't care anymore."

"I called for a car," Mac announced as he poked his head in the door. Something in his kindness melted the knot inside of her, and she began sobbing uncontrollably. Mac went over to the bed and sat down awkwardly, patting her shoulder as the intern left and she released her pain.

"What am I going to do?" she repeated often, shaking through her tears. "There is no baby. I made a fool of myself for nothing."

Mac held her like a rock, and comforted her as best he could.

*

Jane opened her eyes gradually as the first light of dawn began to show its dull gray light. She'd left the farmhouse as soon as everyone was settled in and called her mother from her landline to let her know she was on the way.

It took a minute for Jane to remember where she was, in her childhood bedroom, in her little single bed. Her mother would sleep much later than she, having worked late at the restaurant the night before and then staying up to wait for Jane to arrive. Jane had been trying to persuade her mother for the last three months to quit her waitressing job. She and her brothers were long gone from the house. And they all chipped in to help Mom with her expenses. But at sixty, Emily still wanted to work. "What would I do?" she asked. "Take classes—at my age? Work is what I do, Jane. Just let it be." Jane gave up trying to convince her and consoled herself that at least her mother wasn't working double shifts anymore.

As it became lighter, Jane sat up in her bed and looked about her. Not much had changed since she'd left the house she'd grown up in, the house her mother had struggled to keep and repair. Her old room was simple. The old oak flooring was worn, but clean. It was darkened near the perimeter and lighter where traffic had worn the finish off. Her old bureau, with the finish that had blackened with age and the claw feet, the one she'd regarded as a pathetic relic when she was fifteen, now struck her as a lovely old piece. She would not ask her mother if she might have it. It didn't seem right to ask. But Jane coveted it now. Her bed was a small four poster with turned legs and posts and a simple headboard. Her mother still kept the white chenille bedspread on it along with flannel sheets, which Jane hated because they got nubbly, though she'd been grateful for them last night.

The paint, which Jane had been allowed to choose when she was twelve, had been a cornflower blue, not far off the color Nora had chosen for her farmhouse living room. But with age, the brightness of the blue had faded down and had acquired an almost wedgewood patina. Clean lace curtains atop the darkly stained wood moldings around the windows, a few pictures of horses, and a cross above her bed completed her room along with a small oval night table that stood next to the bed.

She'd not spent a night in this room since she'd left for college. What an austere child she must have been to have inhabited this room. There was a quiet beauty in the simplicity of it, but nothing of the gaiety of her friends' rooms. No frills, no girlish bursts of pink, no posters of rock stars. It was as if she were being raised for the solemnity of the veil.

Jane checked her watch on the small side table near her bed: seven thirty. She did not want to disturb her mother, but she couldn't bear to lie in until her mother got up. She'd already stayed in bed two hours longer than usual. Jane decided to sneak downstairs and make tea. As the kettle heated, Jane looked out the window of her mother's old house. Mark had been irresponsible. Now he would be a father. Jane had no doubt but that he would do what was required in every way. He wanted children, and he would have one sooner than he'd planned and not with her. How would she fit in, she wondered. She did not for a moment think that Mark would offer himself to Veronica sacrificially, but a baby complicated things. And, even though this child was another woman's, she would still have to deal with it—him or her. Was she ready to help Mark? Was she ready to be a parent? Could she love another woman's child? What kind of mother would she be?

As her tea steeped, she heard her own mother coming down the stairs and braced herself. Expecting her to appear with grumpy disapproval for having had her sleep interrupted, Jane was surprised when her mother, fully dressed and looking energetic, cheerfully called out, "Good morning, Janey! Did you sleep well, dear?"

"Like a rock for all three hours."

"What would you like for breakfast, sweetie? Are you big hungry or little hungry?" Jane had not heard that phrase since she was ten years old. Her mother always asked that on the weekends when her father was still alive. Hearing her mother so cheery and using that particular phrase brought Jane back to the last time she'd been a carefree, happy, safe little girl. And she burst into tears. Her hands flew up to try to force them back, but they spilled through her fingers anyway.

"Jane! What is it, sweetie? You're here like a sparrow with a broken wing. What is it? What can I do," she asked softly, her arm around her daughter's shoulder.

"Ma!" she blurted. "Stop being so nice to me. I'm not used to it."

"What on earth do you mean? I'm always nice to you. What's going on?"

Jane's tears let up, but she didn't know how to talk to this cheery, caring woman, who looked like her mother but was obviously an alien implant.

Her tears abating somewhat, she looked at Emily as if for the first time. "Ma, were we close when I was little?" she finally worked up her nerve to ask, her voice quavering.

"Well," her mother sighed and smiled, as she bustled about the kitchen, "you were always Daddy's little girl. From the time you could walk, you preferred your dad, Jane. I guess that's how it's supposed to be. But we were close too, until…"

"I'm sorry, Ma. I don't mean to dredge up the past," Jane interrupted, "but I'm such a…I'm such a mess."

"You're not a mess, honey. We *should* talk. There's so much I've wanted to tell you, Jane, but I could never find the right opening."

Jane held her hot tea to warm her hands up, while Emily made coffee for them. "Okay, Mom, I'm willing if you are."

And so Jane took a leap of faith that her mother, whom she felt had never been there for her emotionally throughout the years, would somehow have magically transformed into the mother she'd always wished her to be. Jane told her about things she'd never discussed with her, about how hard she felt her life had been and how piercingly lonely she'd felt. How difficult graduate school was, and how hurt she'd been when her relationships with men didn't work out. She told her about the Hannons, and the farm, and her job, and Mark. The only thing she withheld was the baby.

She finished, saying exhaustedly, "I'm sorry, Ma. I know you always did your best. I'm just a bad daughter."

Her mother jolted her with an emphatic, "No, you are not a bad daughter, Jane. I could not have asked for a better daughter than you. It's me that was weak. Oh sweetie, when your father died, it was like a curtain went down in front of me. I went cold inside, and I stayed that way for such a long time. When I finally came out of it, you were all grown up, or so it seemed. And, I didn't think it was fair to try to talk to you about my failures."

Jane looked at her mother sympathetically, wondering if it were better not to speak of the past. But as if reading her daughter's mind, Emily continued: "Your father was everything to me, Jane. He was my anchor. When he died, I got so lost. Thank God I had you kids," she smiled warmly at Jane, "especially you, baby." She did not notice Jane's surprised expression.

"Your brothers were older, and they were boys. They were such a help to me. They stepped up to the plate, didn't they? They were my little men." Emily smiled sadly.

"You were the one, Janey, who had every right to take it so hard. You were the baby. The first man you ever looked at with stars in your eyes was gone and so suddenly," Emily looked at her with such sadness. "If anyone loved Ray as much as I did, Janey, it was you. He was your first love. I have never stopped feeling guilty that I couldn't put my own grief aside long enough to hold you and rock you in my arms, so you could keen your little heart out to me. I'm so sorry, baby. I should have put you first, before my own grief. But I couldn't. I failed you, sweetheart." Emily said, her eyes welling with tears as she recollected that devastating time in both of their lives, "I don't know if you can ever forgive me for that."

"Oh Mama!" Jane's floodgates broke as she reached for her mother's hand. "I know you did the best you could. We both were in the same boat: grieving for the same man. Isn't that kind of bizarre?" she asked with a choked laugh.

"Have you ever thought," Emily said as they sat at the table under the window, drinking their coffee, "how funny it was that we managed our grief so similarly? I mean, we both clammed up and went to work—me waitressing, and you! You went to work with all those big horses. That used to scare me silly. I wanted to stop you from going to the horses, but then I could see what a difference they made for you. They were your reason to keep going, and no matter how scared I was for you, I couldn't take that away from you."

Jane had never considered before that she was like her mother. Certainly, they physically resembled one another, but Jane had to admit now that they were temperamentally alike as well. Emily interrupted Jane's thoughts.

"Oh my God, I used to worry about you so much—do you remember the time you road in your first Point to Point race? I thought I'd die of fright for you—did I ever tell you what your brother Tom said? He said, 'Janey's got guts, Ma, don't she?' Yah, his grammar's no better now. And we were all so proud of you going to college and then graduate school. You made yourself into something so special."

"I appreciate that, Ma. And I appreciate that you worked double shifts to keep us together and in food. Geez, Ma, do you know what a hero you are? Single mother with three kids in the worst grief of her life, and you go out and get a tough job like that. You're pretty amazing! You know that?"

"It was tough times all around. But we made it, and we're still here." Emily smiled warmly, as she got up and went to the refrigerator. "So, big hungry or little hungry?"

As Emily cooked up a moderately big breakfast, Jane stared out the window. The morning was well along now, and the sun had burned off the earlier dawn haze. There were no clouds in sight. It was a perfect fall day, the first day of November, All Saints' Day.

After breakfast, Jane and her mother went out shopping. They had some major girl time to catch up on. At the mall, Jane looked appraisingly at Emily: they were the same height and about the same weight. Emily's hair was no longer strawberry—it had gone significantly gray, peach actually—"God's peroxide," she called it.

Looking at Emily, Jane could see exactly what she would look like in twenty-five years. "Geez, Ma, look at us! I'm like your clone! I guess I know what I'll look like when I'm your age. Could be worse!" she smiled.

"Excuse me?!" Emily laughed, "It could be *a lot* worse!"

After they shopped, Emily took Jane to a nice coffee shop in Clinton. She told Jane that having worked in kitchens for the past twenty-five years, she happened to know that this particular establishment kept a very tidy back kitchen. Jane poured out all of her heart regarding Mark, how fast the relationship had gone, and her fears about the future.

Emily merely said, "Jane, if you love this man, it will all work out. You don't have to be afraid—look at me: I raised three kids, and I was catatonic for five years. Love is all you need. It's all that matters."

Chapter Twenty-seven

When Mark left Rachel, he went directly to the barn. He wanted to do what he could for Jane, so he took care of the morning chores as she had asked. He didn't expect Mac at the barn. It must have been after three in the morning when he'd called Mark for a car. Mark should have felt relieved that Mac recommended he send Manuel, he supposed, but he didn't. He knew he'd have to talk to Veronica and today—later, after she had time to recover herself. It was best that at least one of them got some rest.

Since it had been Halloween, Jane had decided to blanket all the horses and leave them out overnight, not her usual practice, but they'd be fine in the field for once. She had said, so full of happiness yesterday—*my God, was it only yesterday*—that if they left the horses out, that they'd be able to sleep late.

He felt his chest ache at the memory of her so happy. Unbelievably, it would only have been their second night together, yet Mark could not imagine ever sleeping without her, now. He slid the large door open on the north side of the barn, and turned on the lights. He went up into the loft and tossed down twenty bales of hay. Then he went out and pulled the truck around and loaded half the bales in the back. Jane had put the horses in various pastures, all farther away from the barn than the near pasture— the one she'd finally succeeded in seeding, thanks to Mac's tractor repairs. She was resting that pasture until spring. The Hanoverian stallion greeted him nickering and tossing his head, eager for the hay. Mark tossed him and his companion donkey six strands and checked their water trough.

He tossed hay to the rest of the horses in their pastures and paddocks and checked their troughs as well. He looked at them to be sure no horses were down, and that they were all grazing. The sun was brightening and warming the morning as he raked the yard and stacked the remaining hay in the aisle of the barn and then swept up all of the loose hay that had blown about. He went into the office and checked messages for Jane. He wrote everything down for her. There was nothing urgent, and when he finished, he threw his head in his arms and sobbed on the desk.

He collected himself, and went to the feed room to get the grain ready for the night feeding. If Mac were still tired, Mark would take the horses in tonight. He knew Jane would want it that way, and he'd check them, just as she would have, against any injuries they might have incurred in the field. As he finished prepping the night rations and was closing the feed room door, Mac walked into the barn.

"Mac," Mark started, "you didn't have to come to the barn today. I meant to tell you that last night."

"It's not a problem. I thought you'd like to know, Veronica is fine, just a bump on the head. Mark, I have to tell you something. Maybe we could sit down in the club room for a minute."

The two big men went up a small flight of stairs to the club room. It was designed for fancier guests to observe their kids' lessons and for VIP guests to enjoy an unobstructed view of the horse shows and clinics Nora and now Jane hosted. At the far end, there was a neat galley kitchen and a well-stocked bar, where Mark now ambled. "Can I offer you a drink, Mac? I know it's still early in the day."

"Whatever you're having is fine," Mac said.

Mark pulled down two snifters and poured his father's favorite Louis XIII Rémy Martin cognac.

"You don't mess around, do you?" Mac observed, holding his snifter up to Mark, "Cheers."

"Yah, I'll probably regret this," Mark said leaving off the "too" at the last instant.

Mac swirled the cognac in the snifter, and took a small sip, and sharply eyeing Mark, he observed, "Well, there's one thing you won't have to regret, Mark. Veronica ain't pregnant."

Mark looked at Mac with his eyes popping and his jaw dropping, "What do you mean she's not pregnant?" he exclaimed.

"She ain't pregnant. The home pregnancy test was defective. The doctors did a blood test. That's it. There ain't no baby."

He should have felt relieved. He did feel relieved. But as suddenly as he knew his life was back on track, Mark also knew he did not want to run out on anyone any longer. He wondered how many women he'd known who had felt just like Veronica—just as angry and upset, but elected to lick their wounds on their own.

"Jesus," he thought, "was Jane one of them?"

He downed his brandy.

Chapter Twenty-eight

Rachel was relieved when Mark stopped back at the farmhouse with the news that Veronica was, in fact, not pregnant after all. "It's a pity Jane isn't here, Mark, and of course she doesn't have her cell. Do you want me to tell her the news when she gets back? Or would you rather?"

"Whichever of us sees her first—I don't want her not knowing the truth a second longer than necessary," Mark said firmly. "And Rachel, tell her…tell her…" he trailed off, "tell her to call me, if she would, please."

After Mark left, Rachel tried to stay awake, but she was so sleepy, she dozed off. She heard the kitchen door open, awakening her from the most astonishing dream… She was in an arena in Jane's barn, and she turned to look toward a lighted doorway. In trotted the most magnificently, startling white horse—so white, in fact, the rising sun shone pink on it, like Alpine glow on the peaks of the Dent de Midi she'd once seen in Switzerland.

The white horse would have been a terrible beauty to behold, but seemed at the same time too wise and wondrous a presence to frighten her. She saw Jane in her Queen of the Damned costume and Veronica in her Morticia costume standing on either side of the white horse. And Mark, Abby, Ben, and Mac were also there, and she too was swept into their circle. The white horse nickered to them in what appeared to Rachel a most loving recognition. And then he danced among them, nuzzling them in turn. Rachel awoke weeping from the sheer weight of the love she felt, just as Jane walked into the kitchen and closed the door behind her.

*

Rachel went to the kitchen to see who had come in and was relieved to find Jane back. She put the kettle on to make her some tea and plunked down at the kitchen island. As the tea was steeping, she told Jane the news that Veronica was not pregnant after all. "Evidently, the home pregnancy test gave a false positive—note to self, always buy two," she warned mirthfully.

Jane was stunned at this turn of events. "Not pregnant? That's great! Although," Jane confessed, "I had made up my mind to be the best stepmother a child could want."

"So you determined you'd stand by Mark," Rachel smiled, "good on you, Jane. Go talk to Mark, sweetie. He's ragged about you," Rachel advised.

"I will. I'm bone weary, but I'll go to him." Jane finished her tea and fixed herself up a bit. She brushed her teeth and splashed cold water on her face. Rachel hugged her as she left and told her not to worry. Everything would be fine.

Jane walked slowly to the house. The bright day had become a clear evening. It was so dark near the farmhouse, she craned her head back to look at the stars. She could see the great wheel, the Milky Way. Just then, someone must have turned on the Halloween lights, and the Hannon's house rose in the distance, glowing like a castle in a fairy tale. How warm and inviting the house looked, its orange glow against the cobalt, star-filled sky. Jane wondered what they would do for Christmas.

Phillips admitted her, just as Mac, who nodded to her, was leaving. "Good evening, Jane," Phillips said. "Mark is in the library. I know he wants to see you."

"Thank you, Phillips," she said wearily, "I'll let myself in."

She entered the library and closed the door behind her. Mark sat in the club chair, visibly exhausted as he gazed into the fire.

"Jane!" he exclaimed as he jumped up. His face creased with pain, he was not sure whether he should go to her. But she came to him. "Jane," he whispered, pressing his cheek to her hair, "I was so worried about you. Oh my love," he shivered. And then he released her. "I'm so sorry. I understand if you don't want to be with me anymore." He paused looking at her intently, "Veronica's not pregnant," he added, "if that matters."

"I know. Rachel told me."

"I'm still a bad man, Jane. I used her. And for that, finally, I'm truly sorry. I will not use you, Jane, or have you stay with me out of your heart's generosity. I'd rather go now than risk hurting you."

"Mark," Jane interrupted.

"No, please, let me finish. I'll clear off. I'll go back to the city. I won't make it uncomfortable here for you, Jane. I swear it. I love you so much," he concluded, holding her and kissing her hair.

"Well, it would be uncomfortable for me here without you, Mark," she softly sighed, "I love you, too. If you want to punish yourself for Veronica, that's fine—I'll help, but let's not punish me."

Mark was so tired, Jane was able to gently press him down into the club chair without any resistance. Then she let herself sink onto his lap and rested her head against his shoulder, her body curled against him. He held her more tenderly than he'd ever done, as if she might break, and kissed her gently. "I love you, Jane," he sighed in relief.

Epilogue

Thanksgiving Day came to the farm, and there was so much to be grateful for. All of Nora's cherished children and their friends and family were in attendance in the grand dining hall: Mark, Jane, Abby and Ben, Rachel, Jane's mother and brothers, Phillips and his family, Manuel, and Mac had all come to the house to spend at least part of their day celebrating with the Hannons before moving on to other obligations.

Robert gave the opening toast. "To all of our friends and family for which Nora and I are ever thankful." And then he turned the attention over to Mark.

Mark raised his glass, "This won't surprise anyone, but as a lawyer, I believe in formalities. I've asked Jane O'Hara to marry me, and she has decided to save me from myself, by consenting to be my wife," he laughed.

"And every other woman on the planet is now safe, too. Thank you, Jane," Abby laughed.

Nora happily wept, and Robert, rarely given over to a show of emotions, pumped his son's hand vigorously. And with great warmth, offered the toast, "To Jane," he said, as he raised his glass and swept a finger lightly and quickly across his cheek, "Welcome, my dear, most welcome!"

About the Author

Judith Anne McCarthy was born and raised in New Jersey, where she began her first career as a horse trainer. She holds a Ph.D. from Rutgers University in English literature and has taught writing and literature classes at Rutgers University and DeVry University, where she is currently a full-time professor. She resides in Doylestown, Pennsylvania, where she is currently at work on a second novel.

In the mood for more Crimson Romance? Check out *A Taste of Honey* by Iris Leach at *CrimsonRomance.com*.

www.ingramcontent.com/pod-product-compliance
Lightning Source LLC
Chambersburg PA
CBHW010642100726
47900CB00011B/2940